Katy –

I Hope ~~that~~ you enjoy the

story.

Best Wishes,

Swinging Bridges

a novel by

Tim R. Teeter

Published by: Delta Valley Press
                       Stockton, California 95203

ISBN: 0-9771514-0-9

Library of Congress Control Number: 2005907764

Printed in the United States of America by
Morris Publishing • 3212 E. Hwy 30 • Kearney, NE 68847

This story is for Sharon who always believed in me
and for Brian, Heidi, and Carol who helped me find my way.

Swinging Bridges

Chapter I

In a field just outside of Renmus, I had seen a bald eagle standing in the middle of a flock of about fifty pheasants. It stood nearly three feet tall and appeared to be in tune to its surroundings. All of the pheasants were aware of the bald eagle's presence and slowly moved away from the area where it stood. As I approached the end of the field, the eagle extended its wings and with one powerful sweep lifted off the ground. In a matter of a few seconds, the eagle was soaring high in the air. I was unable to stop gazing at its beauty, so I pulled to the side of the road and turned off the ignition. I stepped out of my car to watch the eagle circle high above the field. The bird appeared to be looking at the ground for prey. I felt the cool breeze blow through my hair and a slight chill passed through my body. The tranquility of the bird's actions triggered two thoughts. First, how the bald eagle appeared quite often in the United States as a symbol of freedom, and second, how only fifteen years earlier it had nearly become extinct. I should have known, right then, that today was going to be different.

As I walked back to the car, I looked down at my watch and realized that I was going to be late if I didn't get going. I got back into my car and continued driving to Lingen to interview a witness. While I was driving, I listened to Tom Clark on the radio.

"Yesterday afternoon, local authorities responded to a shooting in Hawkthorn. A couple of local truckers, Stan Winfield and Jason Windsor, witnessed the shooting in the town square. Stan Winfield had this to say about the events that took place, 'Well, Jason Windsor and I were working on our truck, and Jason heard a gunshot. We just took off toward the shooter to try to stop him and help the poor guy being shot at. We chased down the shooter and tackle him before anybody got hurt.' Local law enforcement stated that the two good Samaritans pinned the man down and held him until the officers arrived on the scene. A full investigation of the events is underway, and Steve Jones is currently being held in the Perkins County jail in Millsville on one million dollars bail for the charge of attempted murder. In other news, three teenagers from Renmus were cited for vandalism for spray painting the Cougar emblem on the football field in Lingen."

As Tom's voice faded, my cell phone rang.

"This is Jackson."

"Jackson, this is Judge Quinn. How're you doing today?"

"I'm doing fine, thank you, your honor. Just heading over to Lingen. How are you?"

"I am fine. Jackson, I am calling to talk to you about Steve Jones. Have you heard anything about his trouble over in Hawkthorn yesterday?"

"Just caught a bit of it on the radio, sir. Wasn't he arrested for attempted murder?"

"He was."

"What can I do for you?"

"Well, Mr. Jones is in custody. He can't afford to hire an attorney, and I'd like to appoint you to represent him."

"Me?"

"Yes. You interested?"

"I don't know, your honor. You really think I can handle a case like this?"

Although I had already established a solid reputation as a relentless advocate for my clients, an attempted murder case was a big league case, and I was only in my third year of practicing law. The truth is, there had only been one murder in the area in the last twenty years, so it usually took attorneys decades of practicing before they got a chance at a case like this. I was anxious and thrilled at the same time.

"I'll tell you why I called you, Jackson. You've been quite a fighter, and I think this case is going to be pretty intense. I know Ron Butler is the new attorney in the area, and I'd normally appoint him, but I think this case better suits you. I'd like you to take it."

It was the long-standing custom in the area that the newest attorney was called on whenever there was court appointment work. With the arrival Ron Butler, a first year lawyer from Kansas, I was no longer the newest attorney in the area and was no longer called upon for court appointments.

"Judge, are you sure about that?"

"I'm absolutely certain of it. You've proven to be one of the best attorneys in these parts, and I know you'll do everything you can to make sure that this young man gets a fair trial."

There was a long pause before I responded to Judge Quinn. His praise was quite gratifying, and I couldn't help but think that I had been doing something right as an attorney. I finally responded to Judge Quinn that I would take the case and began to wonder what I had gotten myself into. I was sure that I was over my head on this one, but in light of his personal request, I knew I had to offer my services. In actuality, I had no idea how involved the case would be, but knew that it would surely be the biggest case in Perkins County in nearly a decade. I would soon find out that this would be the case of a lifetime.

Chapter II

Renmus is just an ordinary little northeast Iowa town. The population of Renmus is about 3000, and I am related to most of them by blood or marriage. Seven years ago, I left and vowed I would never return. As an eighteen year old setting out to conquer the world, I was certain I was destined for the big city and a faster pace of life. The closest thing to excitement in Renmus is the 4th of July when everyone comes home to visit. Even when I was in college, I always came home for the 4th of July. In the center of town, the city sets up a giant circus tent, which becomes the focal point of activity in the area for the entire week. The main function of the tent is to serve beer to the many people that congregate there, and each year, the "Beer Tent" is the setting for one large reunion of the family of Renmus.

I spent four years at Iowa Tech in Sterling as a second string guard on the basketball team. After four years as a bench warmer, I realized that my dreams of basketball stardom were over. I spent nearly every night of the week in one of the many clubs in Sterling and finally decided that it was time to find an occupation that didn't involve chasing after coeds or doing shots of tequila. So I took my liberal arts degree, also known as my basketball degree, and moved on to law school.

I spent the next three years in Nebraska in law school, which was definitely not what I had anticipated. Most of my nights were spent preparing for upcoming classes, and my partying life was over. During my first year of law school, money was very tight, so I worked nights at a local grocery store, stocking the shelves. The two or three hours of sleep I got each day did not seem to be nearly enough. Despite the obstacles, I embraced the education and the new challenges and graduated with honors.

During my second year of law school I traded in my box cutter for a pair of wingtips and went to work at the Legal Aid Society of Omaha. I was fast on my way to public service life, enjoying the gratitude of the people I helped and who had no other attorney options. Although the pay was negligible, the experience was invaluable. I had the opportunity to prepare cases for trial and was even able to try a few simple matters. The highlight of my time with Legal Aid was arguing a termination of parental rights case before the Nebraska State Supreme Court. My supervising attorney wrote an appeal to the court on my behalf and the court graciously allowed me to appear before them. I soon would find out that nothing better prepares you for the real world than facing seven of the brightest legal minds in the state. Their questions were difficult and my skills were shaky at best. But after the experience was over, I felt that there would never be a legal situation I couldn't handle.

As the third year of law school started to wind down with no job prospects in sight, I decided that my best option was to head back to Renmus. I figured that, if nothing else, I could do court appointment work for $40 an hour and earn at least $20,000 a year.

I had heard that Parker Winslow had plans to retire and that he wanted to be a mentor to a young lawyer who was willing to take over his practice. In early February, I drove from Omaha to Renmus to meet with him. When we met, he seemed very excited that I was interested in continuing his law practice.

Parker had hoped that one of his five children would decide to continue the family practice started by his father in 1914. The law firm had been in business for over eighty years and had represented nearly every family in the area.

"Parker, I'm very nervous about coming back to Renmus. I've been gone for seven years."

"Don't you worry, Jackson. You'll fit in just fine."

"How can you be sure of that?"

"Well, you grew up here. Your family still lives here. People will be very receptive to someone who is too committed to the community and getting involved. Besides, this town needs two attorneys." He gave me a knowing smile. "So, I'll see you in September?"

I chuckled. "You'll see me in September."

After graduation I sat for and passed the Iowa bar, then packed up all my belongings in my Saturn and headed back to Renmus. My most valuable possessions were a bank account with a balance of $643.00, an old suit I'd purchased from the Salvation Army for interviews, and my dream of being a successful attorney. My dreams had been many, but this one was simply to become the best lawyer I could be and to help those people who needed it most.

My seven-year hiatus from Renmus had given me a new appreciation for the town in which I'd spent my childhood. My youth had been filled with baseball on the sandlot behind the VFW, bike rides to the swimming pool at Rotary Field, and exploring all corners of Renmus for any form of adventure. Whenever I looked back on my childhood, I realized that I could not have asked for anymore freedom to grow up to be myself. Neighbors watched over each other's kids, and I could definitely see myself raising a family here.

With the help of my eldest brother, I was able to borrow enough money to buy a house on Pleasant Street. The practice of law in Renmus was just as much about looking the part as playing the part, and having my own house was very important. It was a small two bedroom, cape-cod style. After I had made a few simple repairs and added Mars, my cat, the quaint little place soon felt like home. In the late afternoon sun, I often found myself working in the yard, trying to create something that would be featured on HGTV.

As I walked into what I would soon call "my office" on the morning of September 21st, 1996, I felt both the excitement of adventure and the fear of failure. As my dad told me once, life is filled with defining moments, this was surely one of those moments. Parker's secretary, Jill, had agreed to stay on and work for me to help make the transition easier, and she was sitting at the front desk when I entered the office. She gave me a pleasant smile, which helped ease some of my anxiety.

"Parker said you were starting today."

I looked at her in disbelief and chuckled. The truth is that I was speechless, in awe of the moment and my surroundings.

"So, what does a lawyer do who doesn't have any clients?"

Shrugging her shoulders, she said suggested, "I don't know maybe play computer games for a few hours and hope that someone calls or stops in."

I was instantly drawn to Jill's sense of humor and knew that if she had the patience to stay and keep the office running, we would be very successful. I didn't lack the motivation to be a success, just the clients. I occupied my morning by alphabetizing the business cards I found in Parker's old desk, filling both of the staplers, and recording a message on my voice mail. The office was nearly spotless, and Jill would probably have told you that was the only moment in my legal career in which that has been true. About two hours and five games of spider solitaire later, I walked out of my office and back to Jill's desk in the reception area.

"Anyone call?"

"Not yet, Jackson. But I'm sure if we get some rain, every farmer in three counties will be in to see you."

I laughed, hoping that was true.

"I'm going to the bank to set up an office account."

"Okay. Parker has always had his account at First National Bank. I'm not saying that you need to open an account there, but that is where Parker banks."

I took a deep breath and looked at Jill. I had a deep fear of discussing my current financial situation with her but knew it had to be done.

"I think you should know that I only have $643.00 and that I might not be able to pay you for awhile."

"I completely understand," Jill responded. "I spent nearly six years working for Parker through good financial times and tight financial times. I know I'll get paid when the office has the money."

"Wow, I don't know what to say. Thanks for understanding. I'll make it up to you."

"I know you will. If Parker trusted you enough to help you get started, then I believe in you, too."

Jill's understanding was mind-boggling to me. I couldn't imagine anywhere else in the world where I would have been able to employ someone who was willing to wait to be paid until the office had money. I was also quite sure that Jill would be more valuable to me than I could imagine.

One of the greatest assets Jill brought to my small town practice was her vast knowledge of the family relationships in most of the area. Jill had been born in Renmus, as had both her parents. Her family had resided in

Renmus since 1904, and all four of her grandparents were still living in town, as were several of her siblings and cousins. Her relatives had been among the founding fathers of the town and had owned an interest in nearly twenty different Renmus establishments.

Jill had returned to Renmus after college to marry Tom, her high school sweetheart, and they had been raising sheep and running a little farm ever since. Both of them had jobs off the farm as well to help supplement their income. The traditional family farming community had been ransacked by modern large corporate farms, and the family farmer now needed two additional incomes just to stay in business. The two of them had been trying to make a go of it in farming for ten years, but the current condition of the agriculture markets threatened the future of their farm.

The first few months were rough on both Jill and me, but a large settlement in a car accident came through after four months, providing the office with the bankroll we needed to survive. Within five months, I was representing clients as diverse as construction companies, banks, hospitals, and college athletes whose athletic teams had been discontinued because of Title IX. Eight months after starting the practice, I became the general counsel for a start-up internet company from New York City, which rapidly became one of the largest internet advertisement providers in the world.

The past two years had been very successful, and I had moved my practice from my small, single office confines on First Street to a new building on Main Street. The new building had been completely renovated and had a law library that included one of the largest sets of legal books in all of northeast Iowa. The three offices and conference room, integrated with modern technology, provided me with the space to add staff and other attorneys to assist me in managing my expanding practice.

In the beginning the success of the firm was largely due to supply and demand and location. I was one of only two lawyers practicing law in Renmus, with the next closest attorney located twenty miles away in Bremer. The fact that Renmus was centrally located certainly helped. A thirty minute drive could put me in one of five different county seats, which allowed me to practice in all five of them.

The legal community in the surrounding area was very small as well. A total of fifteen attorneys belonged to the Stoker County Bar, with twelve of them being located in the county seat of Bremer. The Perkins County Bar was even smaller, with only ten attorneys, all of whom had their offices located in Millsville.

The population of this five county area was about 40,000 people, and the economy of the area was directly related to the success of the local farmers. I quickly learned that the success of my business would depend, at least in part, on the help of Mother Nature. When the weather was good, farmers had more money to spend on transactions which required legal services.

I loved driving from county to county which gave me the chance to see the countryside. I had the feeling that I was practicing law in another time and place. I remember when I first arrived back home, Parker had said to me, "The eye of the artist finds the grace to reveal it." That had never seemed truer than in this place and time and in the life I had created for myself. I felt as if I'd traveled back in time, moving to a town that was still committed to the hospitality and social interactions of a period of time that had occurred nearly a half century earlier. During the summer, the one ice cream store would open around one, and all the children would ride their bicycles to get a scoop of ice cream on their way to the pool and another on their way back home. As the afternoon waned, the streets were filled with talk of politics and the weather as people came out for their evening walks.

The only thing more calming than the many small towns I practiced law in were the green fields that blanketed the countryside and the clear nights that allowed me to see thousands of stars a million miles away. The beauty of my surroundings was inspiring and helped set my soul free. I was becoming a man that I was proud to be, one who believed in ethics, morality, and most importantly in his fellow man.

In the evening, like many others, I often walked down the street and visited with neighbors. The routine was very relaxing, since it almost always included a stop at a neighbor's home to share an hour and a couple of beers. As far as I could tell, socializing had been a tradition that had been going on for generations. Around here time passed only at the speed you wanted it to, and leisure was still a way of life. Living this lifestyle, I believed that I was doing something good for the world and that I was helping people with their problems. An elderly couple would come to my office for help with estate planning, or a young couple would come see me for help with planning for the futures of their children. Many times I had the opportunity to be involved in the creation of others' lives, and I was proud to be a part of that work.

One evening a few weeks after I had started my practice, I decided to walk from my house on Pleasant Street down to the office. It was a cool, clear, fall evening and the streets of Renmus were deserted. As I walked toward my Main Street, I spent a few minutes staring up at the stars. The Big Dipper was very bright in the northern sky. When I turned onto First Street, I saw a young couple walking two dogs and I recognized them as Spencer and Lynn Kompel. Although they'd also moved to Renmus that summer, we had not yet met, so I walked over to introduce myself.

"Good evening, I'm Jackson Wright."

"Good evening, Jackson. It's nice to finally meet you. Stacy Mark at the reality office told us you'd moved to town. I'm Lynn Kompel, and this is my husband Spencer."

I looked down at the two dogs. One was a white boxer and the other was a Doberman pinscher.

"And your dogs' names?"

"Well, the boxer's named Bandit, and the Doberman's named Jackie."

As I reached down and to pet the dogs, I looked back at Lynn and asked, "So what do you think of Renmus?"

"Well, it's really quiet, but we like it so far."

Spencer had walked away with Jackie, so Lynn and I continued to chat a bit longer about Renmus and where we had gone to college. I learned that Lynn and Spencer had met in college, and the two of them had been married for nearly five years.

After Spencer finished dental school, they had moved to a small town south of Topeka. Where Spencer had been an associate in a dentist's office.

"So, what brought you to Renmus?"

"The opportunity to own our own practice and be closer to family."

"Sounds a lot like me. Have you met many people yet?"

"Well, we've met quite a few people at the office, and since we both have family in the area, it's a little easier."

"Anyone around our age?"

She laughed. "Not really. Seems like the youngest people around here are at least fifteen years older than we are."

"That's actually true. Very few people that I went to high school with have come back after college, and I wasn't really friends with the ones that are still here."

I looked at my watch and noticed that it was getting close to ten o'clock.

"I should probably get going, but it sure was nice to finally meet you and Spencer."

"Why don't you join us for dinner next week? Are you free on Tuesday?"

"Well, I don't know." I smiled. "That's laundry night, but I suppose I could move that to Wednesday."

"Great. Come on over whenever you're done with work and don't worry about bringing anything."

"Thank you, Lynn. I'll look forward to it."

Lynn and I said good night and I waved to Spencer as I headed toward my office. As I walked, I thought about Renmus, my childhood home, and the journey my life had taken in leading me back here. Although the town seemed exactly the same, I knew many people, but had few friends. Renmus offered few opportunities to college graduates, so most of my friends had not returned.

Chapter III

I had never been this eager to get started on a case. On the way back from Lingen, I called Jill and asked her to contact the Perkins County clerk's office and have them fax over the complaint and supporting documents for the Jones case. I couldn't wait to read the complaint and police report.

When I arrived at the office, Jill handed me a file on Steve Jones that seemed thick enough to be a month old. A large number of documents supporting the complaint had already been filed, and it looked as if it would be fairly easy to find the witnesses to the shooting. She also handed me my morning messages. It appeared that the news had traveled fast. Rich Gunville, from KRQJ, the television station in Cedar Rapids, had called, as had reporters from various newspapers in the area. It was clear that I was not only going to be fighting a legal battle, but I would also be fighting a political one. The people in this area would not be interested in seeing Steve Jones going free, and I didn't know if that was even possible.

Two years of legal practice in Renmus had taught me that the people on the street would be talking about Steve Jones for quite some time. At the Renmus Café, farmers and city folk alike would have him convicted by sunset. Good gossip in Renmus was just as valuable as a good crop and spread faster than a late summer grass fire. In a couple of days, I wouldn't be able walk down the street without feeling people watching me and whispering about my latest client. Soon I would lose count of the number of people who had said to me, "So Jackson, you're representing Steve Jones. I can't believe you are representing that low life." I found it ironic that almost everyone believed in a harsh criminal system, except when it was they that had been pulled over driving home from Pete's Pub after having one too many.

Most files, when initially opened, include a two to three page compliant, which sets forth the charges against the defendant, and a copy of the police report. The Steve Jones file was nearly an inch thick and included written and signed statements from Jeff Jones, Stan Winfield, Esther Smithers, and Jason Windsor. In looking through these statements, it appeared that Jeff Jones was both the victim of the attempted murder and the brother of Steve Jones. After reviewing the file, I decided it was time to meet my client. I walked back to the reception area and stopped at Jill's desk.

"I'm heading to the jail."

"Okay. Have a safe trip."

"Thanks."

As I walked toward the door, Jill's voice stopped me, "Jackson."

I turned around, "Yes?"

"Steve dates Beth Zable, Doc Zable's daughter."

"Really. Do you know anything else about Steve?"

"Just that he works out at Schniders."

"Thanks, Jill. What would I do without you?"

"Hey, I almost forgot. Travis has a track meet today. Is it alright if I leave around three so I can see him run?"

"Absolutely. If I'm not back, just lock up."

"Will do."

"I want a complete report of the meet tomorrow."

"Okay. Night, Jackson."

"Bye, Jill."

I could only imagine the impact Jill was making on her children and their lives. She had three children and hadn't missed a single baseball game, school play, band recital, Cub Scout event, or any other activity her children had participated in since she had started working for me. Her family was important to her, and the example that my parents had set for me showed me that it needed to be a priority in how I treated her as an employee.

My parents had missed very few of my activities from grade school through college. In fact, my father had coached all of my little league baseball and flag football teams. In my six years of flag football, we won the league championship every year and we won the little league tournament four out of six times. He took the time to help everyone on the team learn not only the basics about the game, but also how to execute them. By the time we were nine years old, we all knew how to hit the cutoff man from the outfield, check a runner before throwing across the infield, and reading a misdirection running play.

My father's help continued into my high school years. More than once I had wondered why my father cared so much about how I did. Throughout my high school years my father would wake up at 4:30 in the morning just so the two of us could go together to the gym. I would shoot shot after shot while my father spent hours walking around the outside of the gym. He never interrupted me, but always was a silent supporter. On those few occasions when I would actually put my ego aside and let my dad help he would hone my skills. I don't think that I ever told him how much his presence meant to me, and like many young men I hope I do this before it's too late.

During college, I finally recognized how proud he was of me. It was in Oklahoma City in early March of my junior year. It had been my sixty-fourth consecutive game of not playing. After the game, he knew that I was disappointed, and he asked me why I still played. I told him that it was because he had taught me to be persistent during hard times because good things will come from them and that he taught me to never be afraid of taking risks or failing when I knew that I'd tried my best.

My mother's impact on me was just as great. Even when I was young, she taught me to live life with a passion. I remember the day the two of us first saw the ocean. We were on a family vacation to Florida, and the sun had already set. My father had wanted to take a break from driving, so he pulled over at a beach just outside of Tampa. My mother quickly got out of our car and grabbed my hand. She looked down at me and excitedly said, "Let's go jump the waves."

The two of us took off our socks and shoes and rolled up our pants. We ran toward the surf at full speed. I stopped in hesitation at the shore and watched my mom run full speed into the water and jump the waves. A series of five waves came in, and she jumped each one and laughed. I got up my courage and backed away from the water. Then, I ran as fast as I could to join her. The first wave glided toward the shore, and I jumped as high as I could. I barely cleared the top of it. As I teetered in the water, I looked up and saw the next wave bearing down on me and quickly jumped again as high as I could. I stumbled again but kept trying to jump each wave as it approached me. My mother grabbed my hands and lifted me into her arms. She continued to jump and laugh with complete intensity she showed me on that Florida beach. I have never forgotten how she looked at that moment and how completely happy she was. On numerous occasions since then, I have been able to witness my mother live her life with the same energy. The fact that she taught me to be the same way is amazing. I realized early in life that if I could live each moment with the same passion she possesses, I would be a lucky man.

My employees were an extension of my family, and children and spouses were always welcome in my building at anytime. After school, Jill's children frequently walked to my office to wait for their mother to finish work. Often they would help her with small errands. Travis would run the mail to the post office for us and do other odd jobs to help out. Jill was often able to finish work on time or a little early because of her children's help. Occasionally, I would bring them treats or even little rewards. Travis was a big Ken Griffey, Jr. fan, so one day after he helped out, I decided to give him a rookie card of his hero. After that Travis was even quicker to offer his help to his mother.

The little advantages of being involved in her children's lives helped Jill enjoy her employment better. Her children definitely enjoyed hanging out at the office and having time to do things with their mom. They would always run into the office at full speed and nearly have a collision trying to be the first to give their mom a hug. Each afternoon that they came to the office, the children would leave with smiles on their faces and excitement to be off to the farm as a family.

Eager to be on my way, I grabbed my topcoat from the coat rack near the door and headed back out onto Main Street. An early afternoon breeze had picked up while I was in my office. It never ceased to surprise me how quickly the weather would change in these parts, and a winter storm would be blowing in without much warning from Tom Clark or any other newsman. I walked the half block to the garage where I parked my 1995 Saturn. The garage was an old gas station that I bought for the handsome price of $8,000.00, perhaps the best deal I had ever made. I purchased the garage shortly after I bought the building that housed both my office and apartment on Main Street. It was a bitterly cold walk when the temperature was below zero, but the discomfort was a small price to pay to work and live on Main Street.

On the way to the garage, I pondered what would possess the daughter of a prominent and wealthy doctor to be mixed up with this Jones character. Doc Zable had been practicing medicine in Renmus for nearly thirty years and had always been very involved in the community. Doc was a second generation resident of Renmus. His father had come to Renmus after World War II and became the first resident physician at the new hospital. Doc graduated from Iowa Tech and moved back to Renmus to follow in his father's footsteps. He had never been a client of mine, but we were involved in the same community organizations: Rotary, Lions Club, and the Chamber of Commerce. I had come to know him quite well through our social interactions. I had never met Beth but would have imagined that her upbringing would have led her to want the better things in life. It was my understanding that she was due to enroll in college at Iowa Tech, everyone in town thought she was destined to become the third generation in her family to be a doctor.

I didn't know, at that point, how important Beth would be to the case, but I knew that I should speak to Doc when I had a moment to let him know that I would be talking to his daughter. When I reached the corner, I looked down Main Street in both directions and saw Doc Zable coming out of the hardware store. I quickly walked over to talk to him.

"Hi, Doc."

"Jackson. How've you been?"

"I've been good and yourself?"

"Busy, I'm hoping that I can make it over to my cabin on the river later in the week."

"That sounds like it would be fun."

"You should join us sometime."

"I'll keep that in mind. I was wondering if you had a few seconds to talk?"

"Of course. What's on your mind?"

"Well, I wanted to talk to you about Beth and Steve Jones."

"What about them?"

"Well, I'm representing Steve, and I understand that Beth has been dating him."

Doc looked down at the ground and then back at me, "Shirley and I haven't been very happy about that."

"Why do you say that?"

"He's just not the kind of boy we want Beth associating with. He's been nothing but trouble and I don't like the influence he's had on her."

Doc talked about how Beth had started missing curfew and coming home drunk and that he suspected that she had even started using drugs. He told me that, even though it would break his heart when she left home, he couldn't wait for her to leave for college.

"I'm sure sorry to hear that, Doc, and I understand your concern. The thing is I might need to talk to Beth about Steve. I just wanted to let you know that I was going to be talking to her."

"Thank you, Jackson. I have to tell you, I think that Steve deserves whatever he gets."

"I understand, Doc. Thanks for your time. I'll speak to you soon."

"Have a good day, Jackson."

I left Doc Zable, happy to have had the chance to talk to him, and continued to walk down the street to my garage. I reached the garage and backed the Saturn out onto the road. Finally, I was off to meet Steve.

Chapter IV

On my way to Millsville, I decided to drive through Hawkthorn and take a look at the crime scene. When I entered the town, I thought I had traveled back to the turn of the century. I expected to see covered wagons and cowboys as I drove down Main Street toward the town square. Most of the 200 people who live in Hawkthorn are seldom seen on the street. The town square lies in the middle of Hawkthorn and appears to have been the social center of the community in another time. The remains of hitching posts and boardwalks line three of the four sides of the town square. The town square was made into a park in 1951 to honor the veterans of both World Wars. The few children in Hawthorn often play on the large glacier rock in the middle of the park or in the band shell, where the community band still plays every other Sunday afternoon.

Few people now moved to or from Hawkthorn. It was rare to see a for sale sign in front of any of the nearly one hundred houses in town, as it was usually only death that removed a resident of the town. The majority of the residents were retired.

There were four main buildings in the town. The Lutheran Church, St. Luke's, had been built in 1876 and was the focal point of the community every Sunday morning. It was constructed of limestone and sat in a valley on the east edge of town. It was a large church, that could easily accomodate every resident of Hawkthorn. A limestone cliff overlooked the church to the north and provided the building protection from the strong winter winds. On the south end of the church was a second large building that housed classrooms used for Sunday school and a congregation hall that was used for church programs. Every resident of Hawkthorn attended church on Sundays, not only for the religious gathering, but also to catch up on all of the important local news.

The local tavern, Pete's Place, was on Main Street next to the American Legion building. Pete's was the main place to eat, drink, and gossip, outside of the church. Its busiest times were Friday night, Saturday Night, and Sunday mornings after the 10:30 a.m. service. On the weekends, the bar would be packed with local farmers and minors that couldn't get into one of the bars in the larger towns. Everyone in the area knew that if you were a minor, Pete's was the place to go to buy alcohol. The owner of Pete's was the sheriff's nephew. Quite often the deputies in the county would look the other way, when it came to the activities that occurred at Pete's. Pete's was somewhat of a local landmark. It was established in 1856 along an old fur trappers trail that reached from the Mississippi River to the Cedar River, and it was the first bar in Perkins County.

The local gas station, Champ's Conoco owned and operated by Champ Stevens, sat on the west edge of town. The Conoco Station was frequented by every retired resident of Hawkthorn on a daily basis. The coffee was free at Champ's and there was plenty of standing room for five or six men. Most local gossip and news made it to the Conoco before reaching the local newspapers or radio stations.

The final major building, the elevator, was located at the northwest corner of town. Six giant grain bins surrounded the elevator, and nearly every farmer in the area would spend at least a few hours a week there, checking crop prices, speculating on the weather, and bragging about a latest truck purchased.

If you were looking for someone in Hawkthorn, you needed only to stop at each of these places. In a short time, either the patrons or the owners would be able to point you in the right direction.

Hawkthorn, the geographical center of Perkins County, had a substantial history of misfortune. In 1884, a special election was held to attempt to move the county seat of Perkins County to Hawkthorn. Nearly 8,400 people cast votes in the election, which was almost twice as many people as resided in the county at the time. It was reported that every living and deceased resident of Perkins County had voted in the election. Thanks to gravesite voting, Millsville had retained the county seat by a margin of fifty-seven votes.

In the late 1800's, Hawkthorn had been a center for organized crime. Horse thieves were the main characters that frequented the many brothels and gambling houses in Hawkthorn. The McLowery Clan, who earned national attention for their shootout with Wyatt Earp and Doc Holliday at the O.K. Corral, were Hawkthorn's most famous patrons. McLowery relatives in the area still claimed that their cousins had been unarmed and attacked by Wyatt Earp and Doc Holliday without cause.

Steve Jones was about to add his name to the list of local outlaws. His actions would undoubtedly join him to the likes of Wild Bill Hickock and Buffalo Bill as gunslingers that had hit the streets of Hawkthorn with the intent to kill. There hadn't been a murder in Hawkthorn since 1889, when three bank robbers killed Roger Black during the First National Bank of Hawkthorn heist.

During the early 1900's, the railroads were the most influential aspect to a towns' growth. Without the railroad, the final chapter in Hawkthorn's legacy was established in

1903, when the railroad elected to by-pass Hawkthorn and doomed it to a microscopic existence. Today most Iowa residents have never heard of Hawkthorn.

Chapter V

I arrived at the county jail not really knowing what to expect. As I entered the building, the loneliness hit me. It always reminded me of the way it felt to be sent to the principal's office but for a far more severe punishment than any I had received at the hand of Mr. Plack in grammar school.

The jail was located on the second floor of the sheriff's department. A long hall behind the sheriff's desk led to the back stairs and up to the jail. The door at the end of the hallway was made of steel, which was six inches thick. I could only remember one prisoner successfully breaking out of the jail in my entire lifetime. In 1984, Jessie Backer broke a window on the second floor and jumped to the ground. His luck ran out nearly as quickly as it began. He landed on an ice patch, slipped, and broke his left leg. He quickly sought refuge in Tom Rysner's barn on the edge of town. After dinner, when Tom went to milk his cows, he saw Jessie passed out in the corner from shock. Rysner saw the orange jumpsuit and wasted little time calling the sheriff.

As I walked into the building, Deputy Martin was sitting at the front desk.

"Afternoon, Jackson."

"Hey, Deputy Martin. I'm here to see Steve Jones, but before you get him, can you tell me anything about him or his family?"

Deputy Martin had always been straightforward with me, and I made a habit of checking with him for background on my clients before I met them. This was another one of the benefits of knowing nearly everyone in the area. Deputy Martin knew even more than I did about the people in the area since he had been a resident of Perkins County his entire life.

"Jackson, I have to tell you, I feel really bad for Steve. I've known his family for years. Steve's dad and I went to high school together. You know, his dad was the running back on the football team at East Perkins High. He helped lead them to the only state appearance in school history back in '77."

"I didn't know that."

"Hell of a player. Iowa Tech even offered him a scholarship, but he and Marcella decided that since Marcella was pregnant with Jeff, they would stay in these parts."

"Is the dad still around?"

"Nah, he's been out of a job for a year and has been down in Arizona trying to find work."

"That's too bad. Do you know much about Steve?"

"Well, he's a local kid, born and raised. He even made state in wrestling as a freshman at East Perkins County High."

"Do you know if he's still wrestling?"

"He hasn't wrestled since he was a sophomore. He broke his wrist and was never the same after that. Actually, he graduated high school early, so that he could work over at Schniders in Renmus to help his mom make ends meet."

Schniders is a local nonunion factory that employs about 100 people. The wages aren't great, but it's steady work. They make suspensions for tractors and found a way to survive in the post 80's farm crisis agriculture world. I'm sure Schniders has employed nearly everyone in Renmus at one time or another.

"How long has he worked there?"

"Well, I'm told he's been working there for nearly six months."

"Does he have much of a history of getting into trouble?"

"Nah, this is the first time that I've seen him in here, and I looked on the computer to see if he had gotten into trouble anywhere else. Only found the stuff from yesterday. He's had a good upbringing; his mom makes sure that he and his siblings are in church every Sunday. You know, they go to the same Methodist Church as we do."

"Have any idea why he was shooting at his brother?"

"No idea. From what I've seen of them, they always seemed to get along pretty well. However, I did hear that Steve got in some trouble down in Strong County and over in Stoker County yesterday. Don't know if that had anything to do with it."

"Doesn't that seem a bit odd to you?"

Deputy Martin scratched his head and adjusted his gun belt.

"It does, but I guess boys will be boys, especially on their 18th birthdays. I still remember mine. Travis O'Malley, Steve Jiles, and Brian Thawer took me out, and boy, did we have one hell of a night. I'm surprised I didn't end up in here myself that night."

"Was it Steve's birthday?"

"Yeah, I heard he and Jeff went down to Lingen last night. Steve got into a bit of a thing with Chess Hackle. I guess Chess is still bent out of shape that Beth Zable dumped him for Steve. As far as what happened in your county, I haven't the slightest clue, but whatever it was, Steve was really wound up when he saw Jeff up in Hawkthorn. Most shots fired in the area since pheasant season."

"Did he hit Jeff?"

Deputy Martin laughed, "Not exactly. He did manage to get one shot through the sleeve of Jeff's coat, but the only things he actually hit were the park bench and a gnome in Mrs. Smithers' front yard."

"Well, I should probably chat with Steve and see if we can sort this whole thing out."

"I'll have him sent into the booking room so the two of you can talk."

"That would be great."

"How much time do you think you'll need?"

"I'm not really sure. It depends on what all these things in the other counties have to do with what happened over in Hawkthorn."

Deputy Martin called upstairs to the jailer and asked him to bring Steve down to the booking room so the two of us could talk. We continued our conversation for a couple more minutes. I wanted to find out if any of my other clients had problems that I should know about. One thing I was sure of was that if anything had happened in Perkins County, Deputy Martin would be more than glad to fill me in.

"Anything else interesting happen over here lately?"

"Just a little thing north of Stanburgh. Couple of nights ago, we busted a couple guys trying to steal anhydrous ammonia at the co-op."

"I heard Tom Clark talking about that this morning on the radio. There were three of them, right?"

"Yeah, we had to search half of Perkins County for one of them. We had a tip on the other two and caught them at the scene."

"Never a dull day in your life."

"You've got that right," Martin responded and we both laughed. "I'm going to run upstairs and see what's taking the jailer so long to get Steve for you."

"Thanks, Duane. It's good to see you. Tell Bonnie and the kids I say hello."

"Will do, Jackson. When are you going to find a woman?"

"Duane, you know if I found a woman, it would be a sure sign of the apocalypse."

Deputy Martin headed upstairs to the jail, leaving me to think about the information he had shared.

Chapter VI

About five minutes later, Deputy Martin returned.

"Everything is ready to go, Jackson. You remember the way to the booking room?"

"Sure do."

I knew my client would be anxious to see me, so I walked briskly down the hall and passed through the third door on my left. When I entered the dimly lit booking room of the Perkins County jail, I felt like I had fallen into a classic black and white movie. The jail was still in the same condition it had been in for nearly a hundred years. It was cold and damp, and the sparse furniture in the booking room was very old. In the middle of the room, there was a single table, about six feet long and four feet wide, with a single light bulb hanging above it. In the lone chair, on the far side of the table, sat a young man who looked to me like he had been through one hell of a day. His short blonde hair looked unwashed, and he smelled of day-old booze.

As I approached the table, Steve stood up to greet me. I put out my left hand and motioned for him to remain seated. The first things I noticed were the tattoo of a snake circling around his left forearm and continuing up his arm and the bruises on the right side of his face. I took off my charcoal dress coat, placed it on a chair across the table from Steve. Then, set my yellow notepads and pens on the table.

As I sat down at the table, I reached into my suit pocket, pulled out a pack of Marlboro lights, and set them on the table next to the notepads.

"Steve Jones?"

"Yes, sir."

I was instantly struck by how polite he was. Although I knew he was only 18 years old, he looked even younger than I had anticipated. I slid the pack of smokes across the table and took out my lighter.

"Would you like one?"

"Yes, sir."

"Well, go ahead. I brought them for you. I figured you'd be a bit wound up and would need something to calm your nerves."

He pulled out a cigarette and took the lighter from the table. He stared down at the floor and nervously bounced his right leg as he lit the cigarette.

"Steve, my name is Jackson Wright. Judge Quinn has appointed me to represent you here in Perkins County."

"Mr. Wright, I really appreciate that you came to see me so quickly. I've heard horror stories about waiting around to meet your court-appointed attorney."

"First, please call me Jackson. Second, as long as I'm your attorney you'll see me quite often. Before we talk about your case, I need to go over some things with you, okay?"

"Okay."

"First of all, I want you to look at the mirror behind me. Give them a wink or a smile or something. Entertain them. They don't think we know they're watching, but let them know we know, okay?"

As he chuckled, he gave them a big grin. I raised my left hand without turning around and waived at the mirror as well. It had always been my style to let the sheriff and his deputies know I was watching them as much as they were watching me. The Perkins County sheriff's department had been found guilty of tampering with evidence in '97. I drew out my own cigarette, flicked the lighter, and lit it, as I pulled one of the yellow pads and two pens closer and spoke softly.

"Next thing you need to know is they are listening to us, too, so say hi to the deputy if you want. Right about now he's getting frustrated because he thought he was going to slide one by me by putting us in here. Kinda funny, isn't it?"

"Yes."

"This is what we're going to do. I'll write out a question and then I want you to write out the answer. Okay?"

"Yes, Mr. Wright."

"Please, just call me Jackson."

"Sorry, Jackson."

"Also, Jon Hunlin is up for reelection this year, and he will be trying to gain every advantage he can on this case."

"Who's Jon Hunlin?"

"Jon's the county attorney for Perkins County. He'll be prosecuting your case."

Given that this was an election year, I knew that Hunlin would use this case to try to prove that he was tough on crime. His opponent, Lacy Short, was campaigning hard against him, making a big issue out of the fact that Hunlin cut far more than his share of deals. With his re-election looking questionable, Hunlin was anxious for any help he could get. Just like the other county attorneys in the area, Hunlin was in private practice as well, but he had sacrificed a large part of his practice to be the county attorney. If not re-elected, he would take about a $40,000.00 cut in pay. I'd always thought he was easy to manipulate, and on more than one occasion, I'd proven that his ability to prosecute violent offenders was suspect at best. He needed to look as if he had gotten much tougher on crime and was capable of getting strong convictions.   My new client was the perfect candidate for Hunlin to prove his new found vigor for his position as county attorney.

　　　The police reports revealed that Steve's day leading up to the shoot out had been eventful to say the least. He'd been arrested in Strong County for public intoxication at 1:00 a.m., in Stoker County for possession of marijuana at 11:00 a.m., and in Perkins County for attempted murder at 6:00 p.m. As Steve started to write, his bizarre story began to unfold.

Chapter VII

"How're you feeling, Steve?"

"Strong as an ox, Jeff. Man, this has been the best birthday ever."

Jeff parked his half blue, half primer gray 1974 Charger in a parking lot just past the Dairy Barn and the two of them slid out of the car. Hanging out in parking lots on Friday nights has long been a tradition in this rural area. You never know who will show up to bullshit for a few minutes or an hour. Jeff grabbed two more beers from the cooler in the back seat and handed one to Steve.

"I can't believe we got busted for riding the batpeds."

"I know. Good thing we didn't get into any trouble, Mom would have been pissed."

"So how'd you get stuck in the swamp?"

"Well, I didn't see the cop until I was already past the beginning of the swamp. I couldn't get stopped as quick as you did. When I turned around to see where the cop was, he was already heading toward me."

"Why didn't you try to run?"

"I figured he'd see which way I was heading, and we'd both get caught."

"Well, I'm glad neither of us got in trouble."

Jeff slid off the hood of the car and walked to the driver's door. He opened it, reached into the back seat, and pulled out a football. Steve took off running across the parking lot, as Jeff threw a perfect spiral, and Steve made the catch in full stride.

"Nice throw. See you still have it."

"You bet your ass I do. So, tell me, how are things with you and Beth?" Jeff asked as he threw the ball again to Steve.

"Good, I guess."

"So is she better in bed than Star?"

Steve laughed and threw the ball back to Jeff as he said, "Well the two of them are really different."

"Yeah, how so?"

"Well, Beth. She has this whole movie type love idea. She wants me to caress and rub her body. You know make her feel safe and comfortable. Star simply fucks my brains out. Beth wants me to spend a romantic evening with her before we have sex. Star would rather have a drink or a smoke and just hang out."

Steve had met Beth through a friend in Renmus, and they had been dating for about six months. Steve had ended his relationship with Star Meslin so that he could be with the rich, beautiful, perfect doctor's daughter. Beth, like many young girls, was attracted to Steve's rebellious nature. Even though they weren't dating anymore, Steve and Star would still get together once or twice a month just to have uncontrollable sex. Naive and trusting, Beth, was completely unaware that Steve would ever hurt her. It was a classic good girl/bad boy scenario. Beth believed that Steve was a rebel, but able to be tamed. While Steve knew he had complete control over Beth and that she could be manipulated.

"Do you miss Star?"

"Sometimes, I really do. I hate all that stupid snuggling crap."

"Yeah, me too. You were stupid to break up with Star, she's a hottie."

"Yeah, well she seems to like you more than me."

"No Shit?"

"Yeah, you should hook up with her."

"Maybe I will."

Although it was getting close to one o'clock in the morning, to them, the night was still young. They continued to throw the football to one another and shoot the shit.

In this area, high school boys were very territorial, and any guy from a neighboring town was seen as a threat. Being caught in a town different from your own was grounds enough for a fight, but Jeff and Steve didn't give it much thought. They figured Lingen was the largest city in the area, and they just wanted to have some fun. The only thing that could top off the night would be to have a run in with a couple of the local boys.

"My little bro's 18th birthday. We really should have started drinking earlier."

"Maybe. I'm feeling pretty good anyway. Thanks a lot for bringing me to Lingen."

"What you think we should do?"

"I don't know. You wanna cruise the loop a couple times and see if anyone is out?"

"Sure."

The two of them hopped into the Charger, and Steve grabbed two beers from the cooler in the backseat. Jeff turned the ignition, and the Charger came to life. He gave the engine a little gas, and it began to roar. He put the car into drive and headed out onto Main Street to take a loop. The loop is for cruising on Friday nights. It starts at the car wash at the north end of Main Street and circles the Big C Auto Parts store. If you caught all the lights, you could make it from one end of the strip to the other in about three minutes. On the night of Steve's birthday, there were about

forty cars cruising the loop and the Jones' boys recognized
about a third of the cars. As the brothers met a brand new
Mustang coming towards them, Steve turned to Jeff, "Hey,
look, it's the Hackle brothers. Chess has been trying to start
shit with me for months. Pull into the parking lot."

"What? Why?"

"Pull over, let's dare them to stop."

"Dude, you need to let it go. Beth dumped him for
you."

"Well, she's a smart girl. Chess is nothing but an
idiot with a letterman's jacket. Now pull over."

Jeff pulled the Charger into a parking lot by the
movie theatre. Both of the boys got back out of the Charger
and assumed their position on the hood of the car. They
calculated they had about five minutes to kill until the
Hackle brothers made it back from the south end of the loop.

"Don't try to start anything with Chess."

"Relax, Jeff. I just want to talk to him."

"Talk, then fight, you mean."

"You have my word. I won't start anything unless he
does."

"Promise?"

"Promise."

Just then the Hackle brothers passed in front of them.
Steve looked right at Chess and waved. It was clear that
Steve was trying to get a rise out of Chess. The Hackle
brothers pulled over in a parking lot about a block away
from the Jones brothers. Steve decided to leave his perch on
the hood of Jeff's car and walked up Hester Avenue toward
the Hackle brothers. Jeff quickly followed, and Steve
stumbled a little before Jeff helped steady him.

"Steve, come on. Let's just enjoy the rest of our
night."

"I'm just going to chat."

"Are you sure?"

"Yeah. Just want to say hi."

"If you start anything, Steve, I'm going to have to kick your ass."

"Well, I hope that smart ass gives me a reason to pop him tonight."

"Steve, you know you can kick the shit out of him, just let it be."

The Jones brothers met the Hackle brothers between the two parking lots. Steve stared at Chess with pure hatred. Chess adjusted his blue and yellow letterman's jacket and puffed out his chest, looking like a giant rooster.

"Look what we got here, Chess. Steve and Jeff Jones."

"Doesn't look like much, if you ask me, Ray."

"Fuck you, Chess!"

"A little feisty tonight, are we?"

"Just lookin' for a reason to mop Hester Street with your face."

As Chess took a step toward Steve and Ray moved toward Jeff, everyone's tempers were running high. At any moment, Chess and Steve would be throwing punches.

"Take your best shot, if you've got the guts."

Without thinking any further, Steve took one more drink from his open beer and then slammed it into the side of Chess's head. Steve ducked as Chess threw a quick left and hit nothing but air. Steve was on Chess in a heartbeat and threw him to the ground. Ray took two steps toward the action but was quickly restrained from behind by Jeff.

"This is their fight, Ray. Don't get us involved."

"Let go of me, you dirt."

"You going to relax?"

"If you let go of me."

Jeff slowly let go of Ray, and Ray moved back away from the skirmish on the ground. Jeff kept one eye on Ray and the other on the two guys exchanging blows on the ground in front of him. Just then, Jeff saw Star Meslin, come around the corner with two of her girl friends. As the girls headed toward the fight, Jeff realized that the skirmish was beginning to draw some attention.

Steve landed a right square into Chess' left side. Chess was trying frantically to escape from Steve's grip, but Steve was using his wrestling skills to keep Chess on the ground. Steve slammed his right elbow into Chess' face. Blood started to gush from Chess' nose.

"What do you think of me now?"

Ray looked at Jeff and thought about trying to help his brother but didn't move after Jeff shook his head. He knew if he tried anything, Jeff would do the same to him that Steve was doing to Chess.

Steve stared into Chess' eyes, yelled, "Don't you ever fuck with me!" And then, slammed Chess' head into the concrete.

Just then two city cops from Lingen came running out of an alley.

Ray yelled. "Chess, Here come the cops!"

Chess was lying on his back trying to push Steve off his stomach. Steve was oblivious to his surroundings and was focused on Chess. The two officers quickly grabbed Steve and pulled him off Chess, as Chess scrambled to his feet and away from Steve. The officers pushed Steve down on the pavement. One of the officers had Steve in an arm bar.

"You going to relax?"

Steve continued to try to break the officer's hold and get to his feet. He made it to his knees, but the officer pushed him back to the ground. Together, the two officers fought to handcuff Steve.

"What the hell do you think you're doing, kid?"

Steve didn't say a word. The officers were noticeably agitated that they had to stop drinking their evening coffee and exert some physical activity. Once in awhile, a Friday night meant that they had to deal with a local drunk who needed a ride home, but this was easily the most excitement either of these officers had seen in months.

"We can do this one of two ways, kid. The hard way or the easy way, which is it gonna be?"

Steve was still struggling to get free from the officers.

"That's it. We're going to take you in. You'll be spending the night in the Strong County jail, son."

"Fuck you."

"What did you say to me?"

Steve slurred. "You heard me."

"Have you been drinking?"

"What's it to you? It's my birthday."

"Son, don't take an attitude with me."

Steve was definitely in no mood to be in handcuffs and was still sober enough to know that going to jail wasn't a good deal.

"What's your name?"

"Steve Jones."

"How old are you, Steve?"

"Just turned eighteen an hour ago."

"Don't you know that it's against the law for you to be drinking?"

"You don't say?"

"You don't give me many choices here, Steve. First, you're drinking and then you get in a fight with this poor kid. You can spend a few hours sobering up and then you can see the magistrate in the morning. She'll know what to do with you."

The two officers helped Steve to his feet, and they escorted him down the alley to their cruiser. The rest of the group quickly scattered and that seemed to be the end to another Friday night in Lingen.

Steve continued to be a hot head when he arrived at the jail and kicked one of the cops in the shin. Once inside the jail, Steve had torn apart his cell and had continued to be confrontational with the officers.

"Why the hell am I in here?"

"Sit down and be quiet. You know damn well why you're here. You're drunk, and you just need to sleep it off."

"Don't I have a right to make a call?"

"You can do that in the morning after you sober up."

Steve pulled the mattress off the top bunk and threw it on the floor of the cell. The jailer came over to the cell and tried to settle Steve down.

"Steve, do you really have to make my night so difficult?"

"I want to see my lawyer."

"It's three o'clock in the morning, and no lawyer is going to come see you at this hour."

"Mine will. He's the best lawyer in the state, and he's going to get me out of here."

"You're not going anywhere until you see the magistrate in the morning."

Steve turned back to his cell and flipped the springs and bed frame over. He kicked the wall and then shouted in pain.

"Kid, don't make this any worse on yourself, just go to sleep."

The jailer handled cases like this often. On the weekend, he always had one or two drunks that got a bit out of control, but Steve was definitely more defiant than he had seen in a long time. Finally, Steve passed out and slept until the jailer woke him up at 8:00 a.m. to take him to see the magistrate.

The look on Steve's face and his body language told so much about how he felt. I could tell that he was a very scared young man. Clearly, he had not yet been prepared for this sort of situation. Every time he started to write, he had to pause to steady his hand.

"Sounds like you had quite a birthday." I said, as I wondered again how he could have ended up here after having spent the night in the Strong County jail.

I pulled out another cigarette and lit it, then handed the pack over to Steve, and he did the same. I could tell a sense of trust was growing in him. We spent a little time talking about high school, work, and family. It was a pleasant break from the hard conversation we had been having.

"You have any brothers or sisters besides Jeff?"

"Yep, two little sisters. We all live with my mom over in Hawkthorn."

"How old are your sisters?"

"Jayme is nine, and Sam is just three and a half."

"What grade is Jayme in?"

"She's in third. She's really smart."

Even though I knew he dated Beth Zable, I asked him if he had a girlfriend. "Yeah, Beth Zable. She lives over in Renmus."

"How long the two of you been going out?"

"For a few months now."

"She's Doc Zable's daughter, right?"

"Yeah. I don't think that guy likes me too much."

"What makes you say that?"

"He's all uptight when I'm around."

I looked at my watch and I could hardly believe that three hours had passed. The wind was really starting to howl outside and by the looks of the shadows, darkness was fast approaching. Steve and I were going no where soon, and we both knew it. We had to get to what happened in Hawkthorn.

"Can you think of anything else that happened over in Lingen?"

"Not really. Just the fight and drinking."

"Do you remember any other witnesses?"

"The only people I know for sure were the Hackle brothers, Jeff, Star Meslin, and the two girls that were with her. After that I was to busy kicking Chess' ass to notice who was watching."

"Not a big deal, just thought you might have noticed some other people hanging around."

"Nope."

"Do you remember what they charged you with in Strong County?"

"Public intoxication."

"Were you charged with assault, too?"

"Nope, the officers said that since we were both fighting and since Chess wasn't asking for charges to be pressed, that I was just being charged with public intoxication."

"Okay. Well that's good."

"Yep, that's what I thought."

"Did the judge set a bond?"

"No, he released me on my own recognizance."

"Did you apply for a court appointed attorney?"

"Yeah, but I don't know who it is yet."

"One probably hasn't been appointed yet. Judge Quinn is a judge in Strong County as well. I'll call him tomorrow and ask him to appoint me to represent you in that case too."

"That sounds good."

"Hopefully, we can try to resolve that case at the same time as this one."

"That would be good."

"Do you remember what you did after you went to court?"

"After court, I left Lingen and drove over to Renmus to pick up Beth."

Chapter VIII

After Steve had finished with court, he called Jeff to pick him up at the courthouse. Jeff told Steve that he had left Steve his car and gotten a ride home from Star Meslin. Steve walked the ten blocks to the parking lot behind the movie theatre. He slid into the driver's seat, flipped down the visor, and Jeff's keys fell into his lap. Steve was eager to get out of Lingen, so he wasted little time heading to Renmus to see Beth.

"Hey, Beth."

"How're you doing, Steve?"

Beth gave him a hug and kiss.

"Well, I could have had a better start to my day. I woke up in the Strong County jail."

"Oh, my god! What happened?"

"I beat the living shit out of Chess Hackle. The Lingen cops came and busted me for public intoxication, and they took me to jail."

"That explains the cuts on your hands."

"Can you hurry? I need to get over to Hawkthorn so Jeff and I can talk about last night before Mom gets home from work."

"How come you have Jeff's car?"

"He left it in Lingen for me."

"How did Jeff get home last night?"

"Star Meslin showed up right when the cops did, so she took him home."

"You were with Star last night?"

"Come off it, Beth."

"You told me you couldn't be with me on your birthday, so you could spend it with that slut?"

"Beth, I was with Jeff. She just showed up when I got in the fight."

"Did you do anything with her?"

"Beth come off it. Nothing happened."

"You promised not to see her any more."

"Do we really have to talk about this?"

"I think we do. You're always with her, and I don't trust her."

"I've known her forever, Beth. This is fucking stupid. Hurry up or I'm leaving without you."

"It's not stupid," Beth fumed as she grabbed her jacket and purse, and she and Steve headed out to the Charger sitting in front of her house. They headed east toward Perkins County.

"Steve, put on your seatbelt."

"Come off it, Beth. I don't need you raggin' on me, too. You know my mom is going to be all over me when she hears about last night."

They hadn't gone more than three blocks when they met Deputy Jarvis Simms. Deputy Simms quickly pulled a "U" turn behind Steve and flipped on his lights. Steve eased to the side of the road and waited for Jarvis to approach his window.

"Can you fuckin' believe this?"

"I told you to put your seat belt on."

"Shut the hell up, Beth, it's my damn birthday."

Steve rolled down his window and looked up at Jarvis.

"Afternoon, Steve. You know why I pulled you over?"

"Not quite sure, Deputy."

"Well, you're not wearing your seatbelt, and here in Iowa it's against the law not to wear a seat belt when you're in the front seat of a moving automobile. Hi, Beth. How's your dad?"

"He's doing great, Jarvis. Thanks for asking."

"Can I have your license and registration, Steve?"

"Sure. It's Jeff's car you know."

"Ok. Thanks, Steve. I'll be right back."

Jarvis took the license and registration and walked back to his cruiser. Steve could see in the mirror that Jarvis was talking on his radio.

"I can't fucking believe this."

"I told you to put your seatbelt on."

"Give it a rest, Beth."

Steve saw Jarvis walking back toward his window and muttered to himself, "Please don't give me a ticket."

"You need to try to suck up a bit more to Jarvis, Steve."

"I know I do."

Steve looked back at the window.

"Hi, Jarvis."

"Well, Steve, I'm going to give you a ticket for not wearing your seatbelt."

"Figures."

"Do you mind if I look through the car?"

"Suit yourself, it's Jeff's."

"Will you and Beth please hop out and wait on the sidewalk?"

"Sure."

Steve opened the driver's side door and got out of the car. He walked around the car and met Beth on the sidewalk.

"Can you open the trunk for me, Steve?"

"Yep."

Steve popped the trunk, and Deputy Simms started looking through it. He found a pair of old Nikes, some jumper cables, a spare tire, and a tow rope. Since the car was older, the trunk was pretty big and all of the coverings were missing. Jarvis closed the trunk and walked to the driver's side of the car. He pulled his flashlight from his belt so that he could see better under the front seat. He pulled a cigar box out from under the seat and set it on the hood. He continued to search under the front seats and did not find any other items except an empty pop bottle and a copy of the latest *Sports Illustrated*.

"Steve, I'm going to look in this cigar box."

"Suit yourself."

Jarvis opened the lid and discovered a baggie containing a green leafy substance inside.

"Do you know who this belongs to, Steve?"

Steve, not wanting to get his brother in trouble, replied, "Oh that. It's mine."

Jarvis walked back to his cruiser and took out a THC testing kit.

Beth looked at Steve and asked, "When did you start smoking weed?"

"I don't. It's not mine."

"Well, why did you say that it was then?"

"You don't know anything, do you?"

"I don't understand why you would say it was yours."

"I don't want Jeff getting in trouble."

"So you'd rather get in trouble for him."

"He's my brother. He'd do it for me."

"Are you sure about that? Doesn't appear to me like he's getting in much trouble."

"What are you trying to say, Beth?"

"Nothing, Steve. Just forget it."

"You better shut the fuck up. You're pissing me off."

"I'm just saying."

"I said shut your mouth."

While Steve and Beth bickered, Deputy Simms quickly ran a test on the green leafy substance and found it to be marijuana. He got out of his car and walked back to talk to Steve.

"Here comes Jarvis, so shut the fuck up before I smack you."

Jarvis stopped next to Steve and said, "Steve, I'm placing you under arrest for the possession of marijuana. I've weighed it and it's a quarter of an ounce. I'm taking you down to the Stoker County Jail. You'll be in court for your bond hearing this afternoon."

"My day just keeps getting better."

"Steve, do you understand why I am arresting you?"

"Yeah, yeah. You found marijuana."

"Well, that, and the fact that you admitted it was yours. Is the marijuana really yours, Steve?"

"Are you saying that I was lying to you, Jarvis?"

"No, I just want to be sure that it's really yours."

"It is."

"Well, then, I don't have a choice. I'm placing you under arrest for possession of marijuana and taking you to the Stoker County Jail to be processed. Do you have any questions?"

"Yeah, one. Is it okay if Beth takes Jeff's car?"

"That will be fine."

Jarvis read Steve his constitutional rights, handcuffed him, and placed him in the back seat of the cruiser. They then headed for Bremer, the county seat of Stoker County. In Deputy Simms' excitement to arrest Steve for possession of marijuana, he neglected to search the rest of the car, which I would soon find out was a big mistake.

Steve stopped writing for a few seconds and pulled yet another cigarette from the pack. He lit it while I stood up to stretch. It was now nearly ten o'clock, and we still hadn't gotten to what had happened in Perkins County. I was becoming fascinated with Steve's story. I had never heard of anyone being arrested in three different counties on the same day. I took a few steps towards the mirror and then turned to look back at Steve. Steve was staring out the single window of the room into the blackness of the night. I think that he was quickly realizing that it was going to be a long time before he could breathe the fresh air of Perkins County again.

"Okay. I need to call over to Judge Wilson in Stoker County tomorrow and have him appoint me to represent you on that case as well."

I hadn't really understood the magnitude of the case that I had accepted earlier in the day. It was beginning to be clear that I was going to be dealing with many different judges and county attorneys regarding Steve Jones. The three counties are very different when it comes legal battles. The county attorneys in Strong County and Stoker County have been even bigger pains to deal with than Jon Hunlin over in Perkins County.

Steve got up and stretched his legs and asked if he could get a drink of water. I left the booking room for a brief moment and asked the jailer to bring us a pitcher of water and two cups. I had become so enthralled with Steve's story that I'd forgotten that I hadn't had anything to eat or drink for nearly six hours. The interview had taken much longer than I'd expected, but Steve's story was one of the most bizarre that I had heard in my short legal career.

I poured glasses of water for both of us and pulled out two more cigarettes. We lit them, and I sat back in my chair across the table from Steve. It was now completely dark outside, with the exception of the street lamps shining along the street that bordered the town square. The Perkins County courthouse and jail are situated on a hill in the middle of the town square. This was the highest point in the town, and on a clear day, one could see most of the south side of town. Tonight, I could see the buildings that lined the opposite side of the street and a few cars parked along the curb. Snow had begun to fall and I realized that it was going to be a long, hard drive home.

Steve was really beginning to look tired, and I knew that we both needed some sleep. I asked Steve if he wanted to quit for the night, but he was adamant that he wanted to continue.

"Are you ready to tell me about what happened in Hawkthorn, Steve?"

Steve nodded his head and began to write.

Chapter IX

Judge Wilson sat on the bench, and looking down at Steve. He had been an assistant county attorney in Jones County before being appointed Associate Judge for Stoker County. He was known for being very biased for the prosecution and the likelihood of Steve's getting out of this matter in Stoker County seemed nearly impossible. Over the past three years, Judge Wilson had earned the honor of being the most appealed judge in the area. Local attorneys often joked that the Clerk of the Iowa Supreme Court had the Clerk of the Stoker County Court on speed dial as much as they called to get files. Thirty-two of Judge Wilson's rulings in trials had been overruled last year alone, but due to the retention system of judges in Iowa, he will surely be sitting on the bench until the day he dies.

The beauty of the Stoker County courthouse is that it is the oldest courthouse in all of Iowa. It was built in 1876 and was renovated in 1903, 1938, and, most recently, in 1968. Forty-seven marble steps lead to the entrance of the courthouse. I knew the exact number, having counted them not less than a hundred times. At the top of the steps is a giant archway lined with six marble pillars. Once inside the courthouse, visitors often find themselves awestruck as they gaze upward at the third floor ceiling and the stained glass dome.

At the far end of the second floor is the only courtroom in Stoker County. Although there are fifteen rows of oak benches on both sides of the aisle leading to front of the courtroom, there seldom are more than five or six people present to watch the court proceedings. The Judge's bench is dominated by a giant black leather chair. In the jury box, the twelve comfortable-looking chairs appear to be thirty years old. Two long wooden library tables served as counsel tables and are flanked by the same style chairs as the ones in the jury box. The true beauty of the room, though, is a glorious mural the ceiling contained depicting a farm scene from the turn of the century painted on the twenty foot ceiling. Although the floors were finely polished wood, I never saw anyone polish them but knew that, in their present condition, someone had paid close attention to maintaining their luster.

"Mr. Jones, I find that there are grounds for you to be charged with possession of marijuana. I will set bond at $5,000.00. You can be released today if you post 10% of the bond. Will you be asking the court to appoint an attorney for you?"

"Yes, your honor. I filled out the paperwork."

"Okay. I'll look at that later today and make a ruling on appointing an attorney to represent you. Can you post the 10% bond at this time?"

Steve turned and looked at Beth who was sitting in the back of the courtroom. She nodded her head and gave Steve a look of pity. Steve turned back to face Judge Wilson, "Yes, sir. I can."

"Is that young lady back there related to you, Mr. Jones?"

"She's my girlfriend."

"What is her name?"

"Beth Zable."

"Beth, can you please come forward?"

Beth got up from her seat and walked toward the bench. She stopped next to Steve by the defense table. Judge Wilson looked down at Beth, "Are you willing to post the 10% bond for Mr. Jones?"

"Yes sir, I am."

"Do you have the money with you?"

"Yes, if the court accepts checks?"

"Yes, we do. If you'll go to the third floor and pay the clerk of court, she'll give you a receipt. Bring that receipt back here, and I will release Mr. Jones. Do you understand?"

"Yes, your honor."

As Beth left the courtroom, Judge Wilson turned back to Steve, "Steve, you can go ahead and have a seat in the back of the courtroom. Deputy will you stay here for about ten minutes and wait for Beth to return?"

"Yes, your honor."

Steve and Deputy Strong moved to the back of the courtroom, and Judge Wilson continued to hear initial appearances. When Beth finally returned, he called her to the bench. She walked to the front of the courtroom and handed Judge Wilson the receipt she'd received from the clerk.

"Everything looks to be in good order. Deputy you can go ahead and take the handcuffs off of Mr. Jones. Mr. Jones, you are free to go, and you will be receiving a number of court orders in the mail later this week. If you have any questions about those documents, you can contact an attorney, and he will explain them to you. I am setting your arraignment date for ten days from now, and you will be expected to return and appear before me on that date. If you fail to do so, your bond will be forfeited, and Beth will lose her five hundred dollars. Do you understand that?"

"Yes, your honor."

Judge Wilson looked down at Beth, handed her the receipt, and said good bye.

Steve and Beth left the courthouse and crossed the street to Beth's car. Beth had left Jeff's car at her house in Renmus and had driven her 1997 Cutlass to Bremer to be at Steve's hearing. Although he was upset and angry about the day's events, Steve sat quietly during the first ten minutes of the drive from Bremer to Renmus. Beth finally ventured to strike up a conversation with Steve.

"I'm sorry you're having a bad day. Is there anything I can do to help?"

"Sit there and shut the hell up."

Beth looked at Steve and couldn't help feeling sorry for him. She continued to talk to him, trying to be supportive and comforting.

"Steve, everything's going to be okay. You just have to control your temper."

"You don't get it, do you, Beth? You were born with money, and your daddy has always taken care of you. You don't know what it's like to have to take care of your family. You don't know about not eating if you don't work. So don't tell me to fucking control my temper. You don't get it."

"I do Steve. I do understand," Beth pleaded.

"Just shut the hell up and drive."

Beth seemed to finally understand that there was no point in trying to reason with Steve, and they sat in silence the rest of the way to Renmus.

Chapter X

Clouds had begun to roll in from the East, and the temperature had fallen nearly ten degrees. The crisp, clear, spring morning had disappeared, and the gray of winter was starting to reappear in the early afternoon. A few flurries had even begun to fall, and the sun was nearly completely blocked by the clouds.

"I'm going to get Jeff for this. It's his damn fault."

Beth looked at Steve with concern as she pulled to a stop behind the Charger.

"Steve, just let it go."

"Let what go, Beth?"

"Don't blame Jeff for what happened to you."

"So, you're taking his side?"

"Steve, I'm not taking anyone's side. I just think that you shouldn't blame Jeff until you can talk to him."

"What's there to talk about?"

"Maybe he can straighten out everything with the marijuana."

"You are unbelievable."

"Steve, please."

Steve glared at Beth and was anxious to get out of her car.

"Where are the keys to Jeff's car?"

Beth took the keys out of her purse and held them out to Steve.

"Promise me you won't do anything to Jeff."

"Shut up, and give me the damn keys."

"Promise?"

"Promise." Steve replied sarcastically.

Beth leaned over and kissed Steve on the cheek, gave him a hug, and handed him Jeff's keys. As Steve got out of the car, his anger had already reached a boiling point. He could only being this angry once before, on the day he had caught Beth kissing Chris Lynch and had nearly broken his hand hitting a wall. Beth quickly jumped out of her car and ran to Steve, but Steve pushed her aside and continued toward Jeff's car.

"Steve, please, wait. Let's talk before you go."

"What the hell do we have to talk about?"

Beth grabbed Steve's jacket and nearly pulled it off his right arm. Steve opened the driver's door to the Charger and climbed into the car, nearly dragging Beth into the car with him. Beth tried to reach in and grab the keys from the ignition.

"I'm not letting you go."

"Don't act like you can stop me. Just get out of my way."

"No!"

"Get out!" Steve yelled.

"What if I don't?"

Steve started the engine, "Then I'll drag you down the street."

"Steve, stop. You don't mean it. You're just upset."

"Damn right, I'm upset."

Beth started hitting Steve in the chest and tried to stop him from leaving. She continued to pleading with him to stay with her and away from Jeff. Steve grabbed Beth's hair, pulled her head back, and looked directly at her, pure hatred radiating from his eyes as he started to rev the engine.

"If you don't get off of me right now, I'm going to smack you."

"You don't mean that."

"Try me, bitch."

Beth continued to hit Steve in the chest. He was unable to control the anger that was building inside of him, and he hit Beth as hard as he could in the stomach. She gasped in pain as she lost her breath and went limp.

"See, you stupid bitch. Don't fuck with me."

As Beth lay across Steve's lap crying, she pleaded with him not to go.

Steve pushed Beth out of the car, and she fell to the ground. He slammed the door and put the car in gear. Beth lay in the road crying and sobbed, "Steve, I love you. Please, don't do this. Don't make things worse."

As Steve started to pull away from the curb, he rolled down the window, looked back at Beth lying in the road, and yelled at her, "Girl, you know better than to fuck with me."

"Steve, don't do anything stupid. Please, Steve. I love you."

Steve hit the gas and sped east out of Renmus. Hawkthorn was about twenty minutes away, but at this pace, Steve would be there in no more than fifteen minutes. About two miles outside of Hawkthorn, Steve slowed the Charger and pulled to a stop on the side of the highway, gloating to himself, "Fuck you, Deputy Simms. Nice search." Steve opened the glove box and pulled out a .22 caliber pistol. He checked to make sure it was loaded and, with the pistol lying in his lap, finished the drive to Hawkthorn.

Chapter XI

As Steve drove up Main Street to the town square, he saw Jeff sitting on a park bench, smoking a cigarette. Steve parked Jeff's car in front of their house and waited a minute before he got out of the car. He turned away from Jeff, placed the pistol inside the waistband of his jeans, and pulled his Motley Crew t-shirt down to cover it. He then started walking across the town square toward Jeff. Jeff didn't move from his bench except to look up at Steve and yell to him.

"Where the hell have you been all day?"

"What the hell do you care?"

"Come on, bro, let's talk about how awesome last night was."

"Fuck you, Jeff. I got arrested last night and just took the fucking rap for you over in Stoker County, too."

Steve was still about a hundred yards from Jeff. He stopped and pulled the pistol from his jeans. Jeff slowly got to his feet and started to walk around to the back of the bench, while he looked anxiously back at Steve.

"Steve, relax. Put down the gun."

"Why should I?"

"Steve, I'm your brother. You don't want to hurt me."

As the sound of the first shot rang through the air, Steve yelled back at Jeff.

"Why the hell didn't you tell me you had pot in your car."

Jeff yelled back, "What the hell are you talking about?"

"The pot under the front seat."

"I don't know what you're talking about Steve."

"Come off it, Jeff."

"Seriously, I don't!"

Nearby, Stan Winfield and Jason Windsor were working on one of the two Freightliners they owned. Jason heard the pop from a gun, jumped out from under the hood and looked to see what was going on. Steve started to walk slowly toward Jeff, still pointing the .22 in his direction. The first shot had been fired to the left of Jeff, and Steve was still taking aim at his brother. Stan and Jason started running toward Steve, their wrenches still in their hands. From across the square, Esther Smithers heard the commotion and glanced out her front window to see what was going on. She saw that something had destroyed her favorite gnome, grabbed her phone and called "9-1-1." Jeff Jones had taken cover behind the park bench and was trying to calm his brother down. Another shot was fired, this time hitting the top of the park bench and splintering the wood in all directions. Steve had not yet noticed that Stan and Jason were closing in on him. Steve shouted at Jeff as a third shot was fired.

"God dammit, Jeff! You've gotten me in so much trouble today."

The third shot went through the park bench and the left arm of Jeff's coat. He was lucky that he was wearing a baggy style and the bullet merely passed through the material and missed him.

"What the hell, Steve! You shot my sleeve!" Jeff collapsed to the ground in fear and lay motionless, behind the park bench.

Just after the third shot, Jason smacked Steve's right arm with a five-eighths inch wrench he was carrying. The pistol went flying to Steve's left, and Jason grabbed it as Steve fell to the ground. With his arm throbbing, Steve quickly got to his feet and ran toward the Charger. Steve's only concern was to get out of town as fast as possible. Jason, with the pistol in his hand, was in fast pursuit of Steve and closing on him.

"Stop!"

Steve paid little attention to Jason's announcement and stayed focused on making it to the Charger.

"Screw you," Steve yelled at Jason.

Stan, who had been about fifteen feet behind Jason, cut Steve off and tackled him at full speed. Stan looked like a linebacker hitting a quarterback, and there was a mind numbing crunch when they collided. The two of them hit the ground and started to wrestle. Steve made another attempt to get to his feet, as Stan was shaking off the pain of the impact.

"What the hell was that for?"

"Kid, you need to settle down."

Stan quickly grabbed hold of Steve's shirt and pulled him back to the ground. Stan, who weighed nearly two hundred and fifty pounds, was able to quickly pin Steve to the ground. Steve continued flailing, trying to break Stan's hold but realized that Stan had more than a hundred pounds on him and escape was going to be impossible.

"Let go of me!"

"I'm not letting go of you until the cops get here!"

Steve tried to kick Stan and then reached his head up and bit Stan's left arm. Stan let go momentarily and shook his arm in pain. He then grabbed hold of Steve and flipped him onto his stomach. Pushing Steve's face hard into the ground, Stan said, "Kid, I've had about enough of you."

"Fuck you."

Jeff charged to where his brother was pinned and kicked Steve once in the head to get his attention.

"What the hell was that for, Steve?"

"Fuck you, Jeff."

"You could have killed me!"

"I wanted to!"

"What the hell for?"

In the distance, Steve could hear the sound of fast-approaching sirens. As the two brothers continued to yell, Jeff took another jab at Steve while he was lying on the ground. Jason looked at Jeff with a scowl, and Jeff seemed to realize it might not be wise to mess with the man with the gun.

"You deserve it after all I've been through today because of you."

"Quit your bitchin' and tell me what happened."

"I just got arrested again 'cause of you."

"What the hell are you talking about?"

"The marijuana in the Charger."

"Steve, I have no idea what you're talking about."

"Come off it, Jeff! It was under the driver's seat."

Just then, the first of three cruisers came flying down Main Street toward the town square. The second two were not far behind, and the officers were anticipating an altercation. The first cruiser jumped the curb and headed straight across the park toward the commotion. The second and third cruisers followed suit. Deputy Kerns, in the third cruiser, had to swerve to miss Deputy Martin's car as it abruptly stopped in front of him. All three of the officers jumped from their cars with their guns drawn.

Deputy Martin shouted, "Everyone on the ground!"

Jeff quickly hit the ground. Jason remained standing and lifted the gun to show the officers.

"I've got the gun," Jason yelled.

Deputy Martin urgently yelled, "Set the gun on the ground and slowly take ten large steps to your left."

"It's not mine," Said Jason frantically.

"I don't care. Put it on the ground and back away. I want you on the ground right now!"

Jason set the gun on the ground, quickly backed away and dropped to the ground with his hands over his head.

Deputy Martin raced to where the gun was lying and picked it up.

Stan wasn't about to let go of Steve.

Deputy Martin shouted, "What the hell is going on here?"

Stan quickly responded, "This punk was shooting at that guy over there."

Deputy Harms, with his gun pointed at Steve, quickly moved to where Stan was holding Steve on the ground.

"Everyone just relax."

Deputy Kerns motioned for Stan to move, and Stan rolled off Steve. Deputy Kerns grabbed Steve from behind and quickly had him in handcuffs.

"You're under arrest," announced Deputy Harms.

"Really?"

"Don't be a smartass, kid."

"You have the right to remain silent. Anything you say can and will be used against in a court of law."

"Fuck you."

"You have the right to an attorney. If you cannot afford an attorney, one will be appointed for you."

Deputy Harms finished reading Steve his Miranda rights and helped him to his feet. Steve stumbled as Deputy Harms dragged him toward the police cruisers.

"Fuck you, Jeff!" Steve shouted, one last time.

As Deputy Harms transported Steve to the Perkins County jail, Steve reflected on his day. Three different county jails for three different crimes, each one worse than the one before. Steve realized that his last fit of rage had him in quite a jam.

Chapter XII

I looked across the table at Steve, who still looked like a frightened young boy. I wanted to promise Steve that everything would be okay, but I knew that it was going to take a miracle to keep him out of the state penitentiary.

"Steve, I'm going to do the best I can for you, but you're in a lousy bargaining position. Over in Stoker County, the deputy made a legal stop, pulling you over for not wearing your seatbelt. You consented for him to search the car and admitted the marijuana was yours."

"It was really Jeff's."

"I know that, but you admitted it was yours. If Jeff denies that it's his, that is going to be very damaging evidence against you. Can you see how that might be a problem?"

"I can."

"Good. Here in Perkins County, you have at least three, maybe four, eye witnesses that potentially will claim they saw you shooting at Jeff. I think that if this goes to trial, we'll have an uphill battle. The county attorney still has to prove a motive and a few other things and honestly, things don't look real good when you're caught with a gun and there have been shots fired. Plus, the witnesses heard you tell Jeff that you wanted to kill him. None of this helps your case."

Although I knew that Jon Hunlin would not want to lose this case and cost himself the county attorney position, I was not about to give Steve false hope at this point. I knew there was a possibility of working a good plea agreement but kept it to myself.

"Jackson, I'm really sorry."

"Steve, I know you are, but you can't threaten someone with a gun just because you're mad at him."

"I know, but I was just so fuckin' mad at Jeff."

I nodded my head in agreement.

"Is there anything else that happened that I should know about?"

"I can't think of anything. That's pretty much everything."

"Well, if you think of anything else, write it down, and we can talk about it."

"Will do."

"Also, I just want to warn you not to talk to anybody about this while you're in jail."

"Why is that?"

"Well, any admissions that you make in here can be used against you at trial, and every inmate is looking for something to help his own case. So, just watch who you talk to and what you talk to them about, okay?"

"Yes, sir."

"Good. Well, it's really late, and I should probably be heading home."

"Thanks for coming to see me, Jackson."

I stood up and gathered my belongings, including the three yellow notepads that Steve and I had filled with information about the events that had occurred. I walked to the window and saw that a good two inches of snow had fallen and that the wind was blowing much harder. I felt anxious about the snow drifts I was sure to encounter out in the country and knew my drive back to Renmus would be long and difficult.

"Steve, I'll be in touch with you. I'll have a number of documents for you to fill out. The sooner we get those out of the way, the sooner we can get moving on your cases."

"Thanks again, Jackson."

"Hang out here a second, Steve. I have to grab the jailer."

I ducked my head out of the booking room and yelled down the hall for the night jailer. He quickly came down the hall to the booking room and met me in the hallway.

"Steve and I are done, Jim. He's ready to go back upstairs."

"Okay, Jackson. Have a safe drive home."

Jim came out of the booking room with Steve. Steve had been placed in handcuffs yet again, and Jim was holding onto Steve's left arm. I looked up at both of them.

"I'll just let myself out, Jim."

I headed down the hall and back out into the bitter cold of northeast Iowa in March. Out in the parking lot, I hopped into my car and rationalized that the long drive would give me plenty of time to reflect on what Steve had just told me. I was eager to analyze the entire case as quickly as possible, but when I pulled out into the snow, Eric Clapton was singing on the stereo. As I listened to him sing about love and beauty, I fell into a small trance and let my car take me home the way it had a thousand times before.

Chapter XIII

I spent the next few weeks talking to the witnesses to the shooting, starting with Jeff Jones. Late on the Thursday afternoon after Steve was arrested, I headed out to Hawkthorn to interview Jeff.

When I knocked on the Jones' door, Marcella answered.

"Hi, you must be Marcella?"

"Yes, I am."

"I'm Jackson Wright, Steve's attorney."

"Oh. Nice to meet you, Mr. Wright. How are you doing?"

"I'm doing fine, thank you, and you can call me Jackson. I'm here to talk with Jeff. Does he happen to be around?"

"Yes, he just got back from work. I'll go get him."

Marcella left me standing on the front porch but left the door to the house open. I could hear the nightly news and the latest weather report. I smiled to myself, thinking that being the weatherman around here would be a great job. The weathermen get the weather wrong more than half the time, but still get paid to make a guess about it.

After a couple of minutes, Jeff came to the door. He was about six feet tall slightly shorter than I. He had dark hair that was neatly cut, deep brown eyes, and was wearing a heavily stained Conoco Station work shirt. He greeted me with a pleasant smile.

"Jeff?"

"Yes, sir."

"I'm Jackson Wright. Thanks for meeting with me. Do you mind if we go for a walk?"

"That sounds good. If we stayed here, it would only upset my mom."

The two of us walked down the steps of the porch and headed up the block. I looked straight ahead and saw the town square filling with children who were playing in the park. I surmised that school must have just let out. Jeff glanced over at the park as well.

"You see that rock over there?"

I looked across the park to where Jeff was pointing. There was a massive rock that was nearly the size of a baseball infield. It stood about six feet high, and I could see a few kids climbing on it.

"Looks like a great alternative to a jungle gym," I said.

"It is. Steve and I used to climb on that when we were kids. We spent hours trying to push each other off it."

"Anyone ever get hurt?"

"Nah, just a few bruises. It's not high enough for anyone to get seriously hurt."

We continued walking and talking about Hawkthorn and his childhood. It seemed to me that he and Steve had been quite the duo. Jeff pointed out the various buildings they'd sneaked into or climbed on top of at night and told me about numerous other random juvenile parks they'd committed.

"There used to be a pop machine that sat over there."

Jeff pointed to the front of the American Legion building as we passed it on the opposite side of the street. I stopped and took a closer look at where Jeff was pointing.

I asked Jeff what had happened to it, knowing that he and Steve must have had something to do with its appearance.

"Steve did the coolest thing to it about three months ago. At the time, he was really into building pipe bombs. He must have had ten or eleven of them in our bedroom."

"Didn't your mom ever see them?"

"Nah, our bedroom is in the basement, and she never comes down there."

"So, what happened?"

"Well, it was a Saturday night, and we didn't have anything to do. So, Steve got the wise idea that he wanted to try out one of his pipe bombs."

"So, he tried it out on the pop machine?"

"Exactly!"

Jeff was becoming quite animated talking about this prank. I gathered that he had been keeping it top secret and had been dying to tell someone.

"What happened to the pop machine?"

With a huge look of admiration on his face, Jeff continued, "It was totally awesome! Man, it was unbelievable. The pop machine just exploded, and pop and quarters were falling from the sky. I swear some of the quarters must have flown two or three blocks."

"And no one got hurt?"

"Nope. It was ten o'clock, so Main Street was deserted. Then Steve walked over to the pop machine and stuck the bomb into the slot where the cans come out. After he lit it, we both ran like hell and hid over there."

Jeff pointed to the steps that led up to the front of the post office. The steps leading up to the front door were about ten feet high and made out of marble. It looked as if it would have been an excellent place to hide from the falling debris. I was fascinated by the story and rapidly forming the impression that Steve was a bit on the wild side. We walked a little longer and finally came to the end of Main Street. We sat down together on the knee-high, brick fence that bordered the cemetary on the edge of town. I looked over at Jeff as I pulled out my cigarettes, took one out for myself, and handed the pack and my lighter to him. He looked at me, a bit puzzled at first, and then took a cigarette out of the pack and lit it.

"Are you comfortable talking to me about what happened between you and Steve?"

"Yeah. I want to help Steve out. He's my little brother, and I don't want anything to happen to him."

"Why don't we start with the night before Steve's birthday?"

Jeff began by telling me that he and Steve had never planned on going to Lingen. In fact, they'd spent two weeks planning a number of harmless adventures in Hawkthorn.

"Well, we started the night racing around the streets of Hawkthorn on our batpeds."

I looked at Jeff, "Your batped?"

"Yeah, mopeds, only faster."

"How'd you do that?"

"Well, Steve and I stripped down two ordinary mopeds and souped them up. First, we took off all the unnecessary parts; the headlight, brakelight, turn signals, speedometer, and brakes. Then, we did what we learned in small engines class and we bored out the engine. We made several modifications to get more horsepower and then it became a 'batped'."

"Why do you call them batpeds?"

"Steve really liked Batman when we were kids."

"Where'd you go to race?"

"The swamps, where we always race. There's a road about three blocks north of our house that takes you right down into the swamps. The road out there is dirt so it's more exciting, and it doesn't hurt nearly as much when you wipe out."

"How long were you guys racing?"

"Only about five minutes. Met a deputy when we headed down the hill to the swamps."

"What happened after that?"

"As soon as I saw the cruiser, I killed my batped and turned off the road to the right. I hadn't made it to the swamps yet. Then I pushed my batped along the edge of the swamp and snuck back to the house."

"What did Steve do?"

"He was ahead of me. He had already gone done the hill so he was surrounded by the swamps. He was pretty much trapped."

"Could you see what was happening?"

"When I was running along the edge of the swamp, I saw that the cop was Deputy Martin, so I figured Steve would be okay, even if he did get caught. And I saw Steve making his way into the brush on the west side of the road, trying to hide."

"What made you think Steve would be okay when you saw that it was Deputy Martin?"

Jeff looked at me as if I had two heads, "He's Steve's godfather."

"Is that right?"

"Yeah, our dad and Deputy Martin are really good friends."

Suddenly, the picture became much clearer to me. I now understood perfectly as I thought back to my conversation with Deputy Martin, when he had told me that Steve was a good kid.

"So what happened to Steve?"

"Steve told me that he was hiding in the weeds trying to figure out how to escape the swamps without being noticed. Finally, Deputy Martin spotted him crouched down in the weeds and reached in and pulled him out. When Deputy Martin dropped Steve off at the house, I knew everything was okay."

"What time did all of this take place?"

"Well, Deputy Martin probably left the house around eleven. As I said before, we'd just planned on staying in Hawkthorn that night, but since we'd just gotten busted for racing the batpeds, we decided to get some beer and head over to Lingen."

I was puzzled as to why Steve had not even mentioned this part of the story and was more than a little annoyed that neither Steve nor Deputy Martin had mentioned that Deputy Martin was Steve's godfather. On more than one occasion my clients have failed to tell me little details, such as this, that are crucial to a case. It occurred to me that Deputy Martin was potentially a favorable witness for us.

"Did Deputy Martin say anything to you?"

"Just to try to stay out of trouble. He told us he knew that when our dad found what we'd been doing, that there'd be hell enough to be paid."

Jeff continued to talk for another hour, telling me essentially the same story as Steve had told me about their trip to Lingen and Steve's fight with Chess Hackle. Jeff told me he didn't know anything about what had happened at the Strong County jail or what Steve had been arrested for in Stoker County. After he'd seen the cops arrest Steve in Lingen, Jeff didn't see Steve again until Steve showed up at in the park in Hawthorn and started shooting at him.

"Do you remember much about what happened in the park?"

"Not really. Everything just happened so fast."

"What do you remember?"

"Well, at first, when Steve showed up in my Charger, I was actually looking forward to talking to him about kicking Chess Hackle's ass."

"Did you say anything to him?"

"Just 'Hey, Steve.' Then he went all crazy."

"Crazy how?"

"He pulled out a gun for chrissakes."

"What did you do when you saw the gun?"

"Well, I started to get up from the bench I was sitting on, and Steve was walking toward me. I tried to get him to calm down a little bit and put the gun down."

"Then what happened?"

"He just started yelling, and then I heard the gunshot."

"What did you do?"

"I tried to get the hell out of the way. I dove behind the park bench for cover. Luckily, Steve, has never been that good of a shot."

"Do you remember anything else?"

"Yeah, Stan and Jason jumped Steve and got him under control. Once they had Steve pinned down, I went over to talk to him. The next thing I knew, the cops were there, and they were waving their guns around. They arrested Steve, and I had to go over and give a statement about what happened."

"Is that it?"

Jeff gave a sigh, "I think so."

"Can I ask you about one more thing?"

"Sure."

"Do you know anything about the marijuana in the car?"

Jeff looked at me but didn't answer.

"You know, when we're in court, I'll ask you about the marijuana and you'll have to tell the truth. If you don't, you can be arrested for perjury. Do you know what that is?"

"Yes."

"So, what can you tell me about the marijuana?"

"I bought it the day before Steve's birthday. I was going to surprise him. He's never smoked, and I thought it would be a cool birthday present."

"So, the marijuana was yours?"

"Yes, sir."

"Are you willing to admit that it was yours in a written affidavit?"

"Will it help Steve?"

"Yes."

"Will I get in trouble?"

"I don't know. It would be a conflict of interest for me to advise you on that. You would need to hire your own attorney."

"I see. Well, if it'll help Steve, I'll sign the affidavit."

I took out a written affidavit that I had prepared stating that Jeff had purchased the marijuana and placed it in his car under the driver's seat. I knew this would help Steve's case for possession of marijuana. We wrapped up our conversation and I said goodbye to Jeff.

Chapter XIV

Later the same week I had a surprise visit from Beth Zable. She stopped into my office. Jill had come back to my office and said that Beth was in the reception area and wanted to see me. I told Jill to give me a couple of minutes to wrap up what the Springer's deed and then to show her in. I was eager to hear what Beth could tell me, so I quickly finished the deed and waited for Jill to return with Beth. A couple of minutes later two of them came to my office. I got up from my desk and walked to the door to greet Beth. I pulled out the chair for her and she sat down, "Hello, Beth."

"Hi, Jackson. How've you been?"

"Busy. Steve's case has been taking up a lot of my time."

"I'm glad that you're working so hard for him. I think that it's just awful what the county attorney is trying to do to him."

"Why don't you come into my office and you can tell me about what you saw."

The two of us walked from the reception area down the hall to my office. I had spent the last couple of weeks slowly working my way through the list of witnesses. Stan Winfield had stopped in about a week ago, and the week after that, I interviewed Esther Smithers at her home.

"How is school going?"

"Really well. Only four more weeks until graduation."

"I'll bet you're getting excited. Your dad told me you'll be going to Iowa Tech in the fall."

"Yep." She said as she gave me a smile.

"A fine school. That's where I did my undergrad."

After a few more minutes of small talk, I asked her to tell me about how she met Steve.   She told me they had met through a common friend. Steve had come to a party at her girlfriend, Jane Dunbar's house, and the two of them had experienced unbelievable chemistry the moment they met. She described Steve as a caring and understanding guy, a side of him I'd not heard about from anyone else.

"He's done so much to help his mom."

"Like graduating early and getting a job a Schniders to help out?"

"Yes, but not just that. He takes care of his sisters. He helps around the house. He's just an unbelievable guy."

Listening to Beth describe Steve helped me to understand why the two of them were together. Even though I still thought Beth's feelings for Steve were just a high school crush, I could see how she was able to look beyond Steve's temper and see a loving person. When it seemed as if she were comfortable talking to me, I asked her to tell me about Steve's birthday and was glad to discover that her side of the story was much the same as Steve's.

"So, after Steve pushed you out of the car, what did you do?"

"I jumped back in my car to follow Steve. I wanted to stop him from doing anything stupid."

"Do you mean you followed him to Hawkthorn?"

"Yes."

I was shocked to learn that Beth had been in Hawkthorn when everything happened. Nowhere in the police reports had her named been mentioned.

"When I got to Hawkthorn, I headed to the Jones's house. I parked behind the Charger and saw Steve heading toward the park. I was freaking out when I saw that he had a gun in his hand, and I was getting ready to run after him, when I heard a gunshot. After the shot I was too scared to move, so I slumped back in the front seat of my car."

"You saw Steve shoot at Jeff?"

"I don't think so."

I looked at her a bit confused.

"You don't think that Steve was shooting at Jeff? You think he was just shooting to get his attention?"

"No. I don't think Steve shot at all."

I still didn't understand what she was trying to tell me.

"Go on."

"The shot sounded like it came from behind me."

I hadn't thought about the fact that there could be a second shooter. Beth continued to tell me what she thought had happened.

"I saw a little boy in the neighbor's backyard. He had a gun."

"Could you see what he was doing?"

"It looked like he was shooting at something on the fence. I looked back at the park and saw that Steve was still heading toward Jeff, but I was distracted by the boy in the backyard. When I looked back at him, I saw him fire the gun."

The complexity of Steve's situation was starting to unfold. This was potentially the break in the case that I needed. Beth started talking much faster.

"The next thing I remember was seeing him fire again and looking at the park. I saw two guys running toward Steve. One of them tackled Steve."

Beth continued to tell me how she was unable to move from her car because she was scared about what was going to happen to Steve. She told me that the next thing she heard was the sound of sirens and that she saw the little boy run into his house. She started to cry. I handed her a tissue box from the corner of my desk and handed them to her.

"Have you told anyone what you saw?"

"I've tried. I went to see the Perkins County Sheriff. He sent me to the County Attorney."

"What did Mr. Hunlin say?"

"He didn't believe me. He told me that they already knew what happened. I told him that Steve was innocent, but he said that I was lying and that I was just trying to help Steve."

Beth was noticeably shaken, but I needed to fully understand what she had seen.

"Do you remember which house the little boy ran into?"

"How could I forget. It was the house just to the west of the Jones's."

When she finished telling me everything she could remember, Beth sat in the chair unable to move.

"Beth, you've been a real big help."

"Mr. Wright, can you help Steve?"

"With what you've just told me, things are starting to look much better."

Chapter XV

The one witness I still hadn't been able to interview was Jason Windsor. He had been in and out of town over the last three months, making deliveries of grain throughout the midwest. We had chatted earlier in the week, and he told me I could ride with him on a grain delivery to an elevator just south of Marquette. I met Jason at his shop in Lingen. The truck was already loaded, and we headed straight out onto the highway. I was really looking forward to the ride-it would give me a couple of hours to learn about Jason and what he had seen in Hawkthorn. Spencer and Lynn were going to meet me in Marquette, and the three of us were going to head up the river to one of our favorite restaurants for lunch.

"Thanks for agreeing to let me ride with you."

"No problem. I've made this drive a hundred times, and it will be nice to have a little company."

We talked about the trucking business and Jason. Jason was just twenty-two years old and had been trucking with Stan Winfield for three years.

"How do you know the Jones brothers?"

"We all grew up in the same neighborhood, and Jeff and I graduated together. My parents have a place in Hawkthorn on the town square, and they let Stan and me work on our trucks over there."

"You went to high school with Jeff?"

"Yep. We used to hang out together. Steve always tagged along with us."

It was nice to be out in the country, watching the farmers working the fields as we passed. In another couple of months, the entire landscape would be a deep green with soybeans and corn. Jason told me about some of their adventures.

"I remember how the three of us used to go to the quarry in Rath County nearly every day in the summer. We'd grab some beer and head out to the quarry to swim and dive off the cliffs."

"That sounds dangerous."

"We never really thought about it; we just did it. I remember this one time when Steve did a flip from the cliff. It was one of the craziest things I've ever seen!"

I was familiar with the quarry to which Jason was referring. It was an old limestone quarry that in early summertime would be about fifteen feet deep. There were a number of different cliffs in the quarry, but the one that was nearly sixty feet high was the main launching point for the local boys. I'd actually jumped from that same cliff a many times when I was in high school and even a few times during college and law school. It was one of the most popular swimming spots in northeast Iowa, and kids from all around the area would jump it at least once in their life to say they had done it. In all my years of swimming there, I had never seen anyone attempt a flip from the top cliff.

"You're telling me Steve did a flip? Off the top cliff?"

"Yeah! You should have seen it. The three of us were out there enjoying the afternoon. It was pretty hot, maybe in the 90's, so we were constantly climbing to the top and jumping. Then, Jeff double dog dared Steve to do a dive. And, well, Steve was never one to shy away from a dare. So, we were all standing at the top, and Steve shouted, 'You're on.' And then he took off running toward the edge of the cliff. Jeff and I were totally shocked when Steve dove head first off the top cliff. We ran to the edge of the cliff and watched. About three quarters of the way down, Steve was over rotating badly, and there was no way he was going to be able to do a dive."

"So, how was he falling?"

Jason chuckled, thinking back about what he had witnessed Steve doing.

"He was just falling with his back to the water. Jeff and I got really nervous cause it looked like Steve was going to land on his back. We knew we couldn't save him, but we both jumped off the cliff so that we'd be there after he hit the water anyway."

"Did he land on his back?"

Shaking his head, Jason had a look of pure admiration.

"Nope. That little punk tucked up about five feet from the water and spun around and finished off with a flip."

I have to admit, I was just as astonished as Jason was. I had never heard of anyone doing a flip off the legendary top cliff.

"The next thing you know Jason and I land in the water, and Steve still hasn't come to the surface. All of the sudden he pops up, looks right at Jeff and says, 'I take your dive and raise you a flip, bitch.'"

"That's an incredible story, Jason."

"Yeah, you should have seen it."

"I wish I'd been there."

I was amazed that we were nearly halfway to Marquette, and we hadn't even touched on the events in Hawkthorn. But I really was quite interested in hearing more stories about Steve.

"Can you tell me anything else about Steve?"

"He always was a dare devil."

"Why do you say that?"

"Well, last year he scaled the water tower in Waterford and painted a marijuana leaf on the side of it. In eighth grade, he stole Mr. Hedges' paddle out of his desk drawer and destroyed it in front of his house. But my favorite was what he did in the 1996 elections."

I thought to myself, "what sort of involvement could Steve have had in the 1996 election."

"Can you tell me about that?"

"I'd love to. Steve came up with this plan that we would gather up all the political signs in the area. So, we drove around most of Perkins County, collecting as many political signs we could. We had all kinds of signs, ones for the presidential election, the congressional election, the state house election, and on and on."

Jason told me how they'd gone from house to house, stealing as many political signs as they could find. They gathered up almost two hundred signs, unaware that all of them had been for Democratic Party candidates. After they'd filled Jason's truck, they headed for Principal Plugleacy's house and filled his entire yard with the signs.

"You should have seen Plugleacy's yard. It was awesome."

"How did you get that many signs in his yard without anyone noticing?"

"We waited until about one in the morning and then we just did it as fast as we could. We each grabbed ten signs at a time and quickly set them up and then ran back to the truck and grabbed ten more until we had them all over his yard."

"That must have been quite a sight."

"It sure was, but that wasn't the end of it. Steve decided that we should move the signs around, so the next night we went back to Plugleacy's house, loaded all the signs

up, and put them on the Morrison's yard instead. We moved
them from yard to yard for the five straight nights. Finally,
the Webb family called the Democrats, and they came and
picked up the signs. They made an announcement at school
about it, and there was an article in the Perkins County
Weekly."

"What did they say?"

"Well, the announcement at school was hilarious.
Jeff and I were sitting in Mr. Fronter's government class.
Principal Plugleacy came on the intercom and made an
announcement about the vandalism to his yard and to other
peoples' yards in the community, and that if he found out
who was responsible, the kids who had done it would get
detention. Jeff turned around and looked at me, and we both
busted up laughing."

"Did anyone know it had been you?"

"Well, people knew, but we never got detention.
How could you not brag about that type of prank? What the
paper said was even better!"

"Really? What did the paper have to say about it?"

"The headlines read, 'Republicans Commit Political
Terrorism'."

I laughed out loud. "That is absolutely hilarious."

"The article was great, too. It talked about how the
Republican Party had masterminded a complex plan to
disrupt the Democrats' campaigns."

"So, the people at the paper didn't think it was just a
prank?"

"Nope. Apparently a conspiracy makes a much
better story than a story about high school kids moving some
signs."

"You're right, Jason. That's another brilliant story.
I'll bet you have a million of them."

"About Jeff and Steve and me? I sure do."

I looked out the window and spotted the road sign that said "Marquette twenty miles." I knew it was time to get Jason's version of the events in Hawkthorn.

"Looks like we're running out of time, Jason. I think we should probably talk about the shooting in Hawkthorn."

"You know, to be honest, everything happened so fast, I don't really remember it."

"Well, just try to remember what you can. I've heard several different stories, and I'm just trying to piece them all together."

"Well, Stan and I had just gotten back from Jensen with the new eighteen wheeler we bought. It was an '83 Freightliner, and the engine was running pretty rough. So, the two of us were over at my parents' house trying to get the engine smoothed out."

"Did you see Steve pull up?"

"Nah, I was under the hood and was pretty tuned into what I was doing."

I asked if he remembered what it was that had drawn his attention to the park.

"I heard a popping sound, and it sounded pretty close. My first thought was that someone had just lit off an M-80 firecracker, but then I heard some yelling and decided that I should check it out."

"Do you remember what you saw?"

"Hell, yes!"

He told me he'd looked out from under the hood of the truck and that he'd seen Steve walking across the park with a pistol. He said he'd seen Jeff trying to hide behind a park bench and that he didn't have time to think but just started running towards Steve.

"I yelled to Steve to stop and calm down, but Steve didn't stop. So, I headed right for him. I left the truck so quickly that I forgot to put down my wrench and at that point was glad I still had it."

Jason said that when he'd reached Steve, he'd hit Steve with the wrench, and Steve had collapsed in pain, dropping the gun on the ground.

"Do you remember what happened next?"

"I ran over and picked up the gun, and Steve took off. Once I picked up the gun, I turned back to see Stan and Steve wrestling, but Stan got him under control pretty quickly."

"Do you know how long this all took?"

"Maybe two or three minutes? Like I said, things just happened real fast."

Jason's story was consistent with Stan's. I knew that Jason was going to be a good witness for the state because he knew Steve and had see him with the gun in his hand. We talked a little longer about the events he had witnessed, but Jason seemed more interested in reminiscing about childhood adventures with the Jones brothers. I decided that it would be best to let him do that.

The last story Jason told me about their childhood, was as funny as the others. Apparently, Steve had decided that the three of them should climb one of the grain bins at the elevator and shoot their bb guns. The three of them scaled one of the bins and looked for targets. The closest target was a gas station across the street, and for nearly an hour, they shot at and occasionally hit people pumping gas into their cars.

"After about an hour, Deputy Martin came out to look around. As soon as we saw him drive up, the three of us laid down on the walkway between the bins."

"Did you guys get in trouble?"

"Well, if it had been anybody else, we probably would've."

"What?" I chuckled.

Jason said that Steve decided to see if he could hit Deputy Martin.

"Steve missed him by nearly two feet, but when Steve fired the shot, Jeff almost fell off the walkway 'cause he was laughing so hard. Deputy Martin heard Jeff laughing and spotted the three of us up on the walkway. Then, he yelled for us to come down."

When the three of them came down from the grain bin, Deputy Martin grabbed Steve and Jeff and yelled to me that I should probably get home.

"He marched the two of them to their house. I don't know what happened after that, but the three of us never got into any real trouble. I think that they probably got a good beating from Chris."

When we arrived at Marquette, I thanked Jason for the ride, and he thanked me for the company.

"You've got some great stories, Jason."

"Well, the three of us had a hell of a time growing up. I'm just real sorry about what's happening to Steve."

"It sure is a shame. Well, I'd better get going. It looks as if my friends are wanting to get on the road."

I could see Spencer and Lynn waiting in the Jeep a few hundred feet away.

"Yeah, I need to get this truck unloaded and get back home."

"Thanks for everything."

"No problem. If I think of anything else I will let you know."

"I'd appreciate that. Have a good day, Jason."

"You too."

I joined Spencer and Lynn in the Jeep, and the three of us headed out of Marquette toward Lansing. We were off to lunch, and I was able set aside Steve Jones and his problems in order to enjoy the company of my friends. As we drove, we started planning when we were going to put their boat into the water and when we were going to camp out on the sandbar. Spencer and Lynn helped to put life back into prospective for me and Steve Jones's case slowly faded out of mind.

Chapter XVI

On June 20th, I walked into the Sheriff's department and saw Miles Smith, the Sheriff, sitting at the front desk. He looked up and greeted me.

"Morning, Jackson. What brings you over this way?"

"Hi, Sheriff. Just had the verdict in the Rambler case."

"How'd it turn out?"

"Acquittal."

"You're going to have to stop beating on us. You know it looks bad for Jon."

"Just trying to do my job, Miles."

"I know. I just like to give you grief."

"So, how are things over here this morning?"

"Quiet. Just how I like it."

"That's good to hear. Hey, I'm here to see Steve Jones. Mind if I meet with him in his cell?"

"Not at all. Let me grab my keys, and I'll take you on up."

"Thanks."

Sheriff Smith opened up the top desk drawer and grabbed a set of keys. Then he stood up and motioned for me to follow him. He escorted me down the hall at the back of the sheriff's department. When we reached the steel door at the end of the hall, we stopped. He flipped through about twenty keys before he finally came to the key that would unlock the steel door. He opened it, and the two of us stepped through the doorway. Once we were on the other side of the door, the Sheriff stopped and locked the door behind us. We walked up the stairs to the second floor, where the jail was located. At the top of the stairs there was another locked steel door. Again, we stopped, and Miles flipped through his key ring until he found the key to unlock the door. He opened the door and let us through, again locking the door behind us. We walked down a corridor that had eight cells on the each side. Steve's cell was the fifth cell on the left. When we got there, I looked in and saw him sitting and reading on his bed. The sheriff opened the cell, let me in, and locked the cell behind me. As he walked away, I told him I only needed about twenty minutes.

"Sounds good, Jackson."

"Thanks."

When Steve and I were alone, I looked over to the jailer's desk at the end of the corridor and could see that we were being watched.

"How've you been?"

"Not too bad. It's good to see you, Jackson."

"It's good to see you, too, Steve."

"Any news on my case?"

"Still in a holding pattern. The county attorney is trying to weigh out the pros and cons of trying the case, and he told me he needed a bit more time before he would be ready to finalize any sort of deal."

"Do you think he'll dismiss the charges?"

"Not exactly. I do think we can get you a pretty good deal, though. The county attorney is up for re-election, and I just beat him in a jury trial on another matter."

"Really. So, the Rambler fella walked."

"Yep. Just got the acquittal this morning."

Steve's spirits seemed to rise at this news. The main reason I was here was to see if Steve would be interested in a plea agreement and just to make sure that he was doing ok. Jail is hard on anyone, and he was still just a boy.

"Steve, in the upcoming weeks, I'll be talking to Jon Hunlin about striking a deal on your case. Does that sound good to you?"

"Yeah. I'm really hoping to just get on with everything and put this behind me."

"I completely understand, so I'll start pushing Jon a bit harder, and hopefully, we can get you out of here before the 4th of July. Do realize that when I say 'out of here,' I mean out of this facility? I suspect that you'll probably have to do some time, but I'll try to have that served at a halfway house."

"Thanks."

Once we'd taken care of business, I still had about five minutes to kill before the Sheriff returned.

"Steve, I've heard quite a bit about you from the witnesses."

"Oh, yeah. Like what?"

"I've heard that you like to race batpeds, jump off cliffs, and are quite the planner."

"Must've talked with Jeff."

"Yep. I've actually talked to all the witnesses."

"Really?"

"Yeah. I have some questions to ask you. I want to clarify a few things. A couple weeks ago, Beth Zabel came to see me."

"How's Beth? I really miss her."

"She seems to be pretty upset. Did you know that she was in Hawkthorn when you got arrested?"

"What?"

"Yeah, she told me that she followed you to the park. There is one more thing she told me. She thinks you didn't shot at your brother."

Steve stared at me with his eyes wide open.

"Do you remember shooting the gun, Steve?"

"I don't know for sure. I just know that Deputy Martin said he found bullets and that there were empty shells in the gun. So, I figured I must've shot the gun."

"Just so you know, I'm going to be interviewing one more person and hopefully, after that I'll have a clear picture of what happened."

"Sounds good, Jackson."

I stood up and walked to the edge of the cell to look for the Sheriff. There was still no sign of him.

"This information might change your whole case."

Steve started to get excited. "Really?"

"Yes, really, but remember it's just a lead and right now it's nothing more than that."

"I know, but it gives me hope."

I felt really bad seeing Steve struggle to piece together what happened.

"I need you to try to remember if you fired the gun."

"Okay."

"Thanks."

Finally, the Sheriff returned and asked if we were finished. I said that we were. I said, goodbye to Steve and followed Miles back out of the jail and into the sheriff's department. The two of us stopped at his desk and chatted for a few moments before I headed home. We said good bye, and I walked out to my faithful Saturn and took off for the office.

Chapter XVII

"How's the Jones case coming along?"

"We seem to be at a stand still."

"Why do you say that?"

"Jon Hunlin and I haven't been able to agree on a plea bargain. Looks as if we might be going to trial."

"Do you have a trial date?"

"October 23, but I think that we might have something worked out before then."

Spencer and I had been driving to Lansing. We were heading to the Mississippi River to put his boat in for the summer. The spring weather was warming up and soon we would be on the water nearly every weekend, skiing and camping on the banks. Today, however, we would just hang out on the river and then return to Renmus in the evening.

Spencer had become a good friend and a great sounding board, and it was nice to have another twenty-something in Renmus to hang out with.

"Everything all right, Jackson?"

"Yeah, just thinking about work."

"Well, get your mind off work. We're going to drop the boat in and go for a cruise up the river."

"Sounds good."

Late spring was a beautiful time on the Mississippi River. The trees were starting to bloom and barges were beginning their long summer of operating on the river. The Mississippi was a highway for interstate commerce for nearly eight months of the year. The river was lined with a complex series of locks and dams that allowed the Army Corps of Engineers to stabilize the depth of the channel. Spencer had pulled the Jeep and trailer into the state park and I asked him what time Lynn was joining us.

"She should be at the slip when we get to the marina with the boat."

Spencer hopped out of the Jeep, unhooked the trailer lights, placed the plug in the boat, and took out the engine braces. I spent a few minutes removing the boat cover and placing it in the back of the Jeep. After the boat was prepared, Spencer backed the trailer into the water. He then hopped out and asked me to take the driver's seat. Spencer unhooked the boat and pushed it into the water.

"Why don"t you pull the trailer out and park the Jeep. We'll have Lynn drop us off after we get back to the marina tonight."

"Okay. You want me to grab the keys?"

"Yeah, go ahead and lock the Jeep."

"I'll be right back."

I drove the Jeep back up to the parking area and parked it. After locking the doors, I ran down to the boat ramp. Spencer had the boat running. I hopped in and gave us a push off the dock.

"Any idea where we're going?"

"Just figured we could hit a sandbar and drink a few beers until dinner and then head to Sherman's for some pizza."

"Okay."

Spencer looked over at me with concern.

"Dude, you need to relax. Maybe I need to take you to the strip club."

I laughed as we headed into the main channel of the river. Spencer was right, of course. The stress of the office was wearing on me, and I thought that it was good to get away for a day and leave it all behind. We were finally headed upstream to Lansing. When we got to the marina, Lynn was waiting for us with a load of supplies.

"Hey, Lynn."

"Hi, Jackson. You guys have a safe trip?"

Lynn handed Spencer a cooler as I walked up the dock to help Lynn unload their car. When I returned, we loaded up the lawn chairs and a second cooler. Spencer started organizing everything in the boat while Lynn lifted the dogs into the front of the boat.

"I thought we'd cook up some lunch on the sandbar, and I brought some snacks as well," Lynn said.

"That's good and all, but what Jackson and I really want to know, is how's the beer supply?"

Lynn shook her head in disgust and then laughed and gave us each a Coors Light from the cooler beside her. Spencer was at the helm of the boat and was eager to travel.

"Spencer, you think we could just float down the river like Huck Finn for a month?"

"I've thought about that before. Wouldn't that be a blast?"

"What do you think Lynn? Can you run the office without me?"

"Do you think anyone would notice you were gone?"

The three of laughed. Neither Spencer nor I had quite figured out how our businesses would function without us, but it was still fun to dream about it. The beer was flowing and the day was passing quickly. We had been on the river for nearly thirty minutes, and the boat traffic was pretty light.

"Throw me another beer, Jackson."

I reached down to the cooler that was sitting between us and pulled out two beers. I handed one to Spencer and offered the other one to Lynn, which she declined so I opened it for myself. After cruising nearly all the way to Lock and Dam Number 8, we decided to head back down the river and set up camp on our favorite sandbar, "The Dunes."

Once we had the boat anchored, the first point of order was to have another beer and then get a fire started. Spencer and I unloaded the boat while Lynn attended to the fire. Then Spencer went to work setting up our gear like a small village.

"You know, Spencer, "I don't think you have everything set up properly."

"You're such a smartass."

After Spencer had the chairs and coolers in their proper places and the fire was going, the three of us decided to sit on the beach and watch the boats floating up and down the river. I spotted a bald eagle soaring in the sky above the opposite side of the river. "Check out the eagle."

"There have been a lot of them around here lately."

"I saw one over in Perkins County the day I met with Steve Jones."

"There's another one over there," I said to Spencer, as I pointed at another eagle.

"See. Lots of them around here."

"I think it might be a sign."

"What?"

"Well, as I was saying, I saw a bald eagle the morning I took the Jones case. I'd think this one is a sign that things are going to work out for him."

"Jackson, you come up with some crazy ideas."

"Shut up, Spencer," I laughed.

I grabbed another beer from the cooler and walked back to my chair. I sat down and thought about the eagles. I really did think that the bald eagle I'd seen just now was a sign that everything would work out for Steve Jones, but I certainly wasn't going to pursue that train of thought any further with Spencer.

We spent nearly three hours just sitting on the beach and chatting. As sundown was approaching, we packed up the boat and headed for the marina. When we got there, we loaded the gear into the car, and Lynn drove Spencer and me down to the state park to pick up the Jeep.

All of us then drove back into Lansing to grab dinner. We spent nearly two hours in Sherman's before we headed back to Renmus. I was glad that Spencer was driving, because I had definitely taken in more than enough beer and knew that I would soon be asleep. As we headed out of town, I started to make a mental list of the phone calls I needed to make the next day. I could hear the radio in the background as I drifted off to sleep.

"Hey, Jackson wake up."

I looked up and tried to figure out where I was. After a second, I realized that we were back in Renmus in the alley behind my building. I shook off the haze and got out of the Jeep. I looked over at Spencer and marvelled that he'd been able to drive home without falling asleep after being on the water all day.

"Jackson, you look beat. Get some rest and stop letting your cases take over your life."

"I'll try. Thanks for taking me today, it was great getting out of the office."

"No problem."

I got out of the Jeep and headed in the back door of my building. Mars met me halfway up the stairs to my apartment. I sat down on the steps and let her curl up in my lap so I could pet her. I thought, once again, about the bald eagle and couldn't help but think that I had seen it for a reason. I had always been a believer in signs and was sure that the eagle today was a sign of what was to come for Steve Jones.

Chapter XVIII

Five days later, I received a phone call from the Sheriff's Department. There had been some problems at the jail, and Steve had been involved. I returned to the jail to find out what had happened. When I arrived, I was escorted to the booking room and sat there for a few minutes waiting for Steve to be brought in. After a few minutes, the jailer returned with Steve. I shook my head as Steve walked in.

"Steve, what the hell happened?"

"Wilkens was cheating me at cards."

I really didn't care if Wilkens, a new inmate, had smacked Steve. I needed Steve not to get into trouble if I was going to be able to work out a deal with Jon Hunlin.

"He cheated at cards?"

"Yeah."

"Seriously, Steve, what's the big deal?"

"I don't like being cheated."

"Ok. Well, I need to know exactly what happened."

Steve told me that, on the previous day, three new inmates had been brought to the jail. One of them was Wilkens Miller. Steve and the three other inmates had been playing poker to pass the time. Apparently, the game had started out fine, but emotions began to get a little high, and Wilkens was getting upset that Steve was winning so much.

"Why did things get ugly?"

"Well, after I won about five hands in a row, Wilkens decided he was going to start stacking the deck. I caught him base dealing."

"What did you do?"

Steve told me that he'd knocked the cards out of Wilkens' hand. Wilkens then shoved the table, and it hit Steve. Steve had been knocked to the ground by the force of the table. He then jumped to his feet and charged Wilkens. The two of them exchanged a few punches before the jailer was able to come in and break things up.

"So, he shoved the table, and it hit you?"

"Yeah. He's lucky the jailer came when he did. I would have beat the shit out of him."

"You're not helping matters."

I was having a very difficult time getting Steve to understand that just because he was already in jail, didn't mean that he couldn't get into more trouble.

"I'm telling you, Jackson. No one treats me that way."

"I don't blame you for sticking up for yourself. I just want you to try to watch your temper. Hunlin is going to love it when he hears that you were in here causing problems. You're lucky that you didn't get charged with assault for hitting Wilkens."

"Has anything else happened that I need to know about?"

"No. This is the only thing I've gotten in trouble for since I've been here."

"I know this is the only thing you have gotten in trouble for, but have you done anything else?"

"No."

Steve looked a bit calmer. I talked to him about the importance of being on his best behavior while he was in jail. I reminded him that Judge Quinn frowned on people that caused problems for the jailers and that he would remember such behavior at trial or sentencing. He seemed to understand that my advice was meant to help him, and Steve agreed that he would try to do a better job of getting along with everyone and not causing any more problems while he was in jail.

I looked over at him and asked, "Have you thought about what happened in the park as I asked?"

"I've tried to, but I just keep thinking that I must have shot the gun."

"Are you sure?"

"No, but I don't know how else it could've happened."

"I'm going to meet with the witness I told you about. I think that he might have a few of the answers we're looking for. If he says what I think he's going to say, then you'll have a very good case."

"Really? It's that good?"

"Maybe. I'll keep you posted."

"Please do."

I looked at my watch and let Steve know that I had to get going.

"I'm going to grab the jailer, and he'll take you back upstairs. Just promise me that you won't do anything stupid."

"I won't," Steve said and then, after a long pause, added, "unless someone tries to fuck with me."

"Steve, that's exactly what I'm talking about. You just have to swallow your pride and get along."

I ducked my head out of the booking room and yelled for the jailer. When he arrived to escort Steve back to his cell, we all said good bye, and I was off to find the final answers to Steve's case.

Chapter XIX

When I awoke on Tuesday morning, six months had passed since I'd first met Steve Jones in the booking room of the Perkins County jail. After I finished my cup of coffee and a bowl of cereal, I headed down the steps from my apartment to my office. Three weeks before I met Steve, I'd moved from my two bedroom house on Pleasant Street to the second story of my building on Main Street. My new living arrangements were an apartment that was 3,000 square feet with fourteen feet ceilings and the best bar in Renmus. It also provided me the fastest commute to the work in town.

I entered the office and stopped at Jill's desk to pick up my messages. On the top of the stack, I saw the message from Jon Hunlin. A call from Jon could mean only one thing: he was ready to cut a deal on the Jones matter.

Although Jon had been elected to the position of Perkins County Attorney six straight times, he rarely tried a case and was usually looking for the easiest way to dispose of a case. I knew that the last thing he wanted to do was go to trial on the Jones matter. I went to my desk, picked up the phone, and dialed the county attorney's office.

"Perkins County Attorney's office. Bonnie speaking."

"Hi Bonnie, this is Jackson Wright from Renmus. Is Jon available?"

"I'll check Jackson. Hang on one second."

Bonnie placed me on hold and the familiar voice of Tom Clark filled the receiver. It seemed that the county attorney's office had their radio set to AM 1020, and they were able to run that through their phone line. Just as Tom finished talking about the Renmus High baseball team, Bonnie clicked back onto the phone.

"I'm putting you through, Jackson."

"Thanks, Bonnie."

I was very eager to talk to Hunlin. I knew that if I could finally work out the details in Perkins County, I could get all three of the cases against Steve settled. The county attorney in Stoker County had agreed to dismiss the possession of marijuana charge after he received Jeff's signed affidavit. On Thursday, Jeff would be in court in Stoker County for the sentencing on that matter, and I anticipated that it would be fairly straight forward. Clark, the county attorney in Strong County had agreed to dismiss the public intoxication case against Steve since he'd spent so much time in jail because of the shooting.

"Jackson, how are you today?"

"Good, Jon."

"I called earlier to see what your thoughts were with regard to Steve Jones."

"Well, Jon, we appear to have the Stoker County and Strong County matters taken care of. Now we're just looking to see what we can do here in Perkins County or if we need to finish preparing for trial."

"Do you have a proposal for me?"

"I think you should dismiss the case."

"You know I can't do that. I need a plea on a charge that shows I'm tough on crime, especially since the re-election campaign is in full swing."

"Jon, I've compared the charges and with the witnesses' statements, and I don't think you have a case."

"I disagree. I want you to run something by your client. I found a charge that I think he can live with."

"Which is what?"

"Well, I'm looking at a guilty plea to felony assault with a firearm. I know it isn't attempted murder, but the way I see it, it's a win/win situation for both of us."

"In what way, Jon?"

"Well, Jackson, I get my felony, and your client doesn't need to go to prison."

"So, do you have a proposal on the sentencing recommendation? That's the key to Steve's being willing to plead to the assault charge. You know you're going to have a hard time proving the attempted murder charge."

"Well, I certainly don't want to send the attempted murder charge to a jury and come back with nothing more than a voluntary manslaughter charge."

"Jon, do you really think you can even get that? He didn't fire the gun, so the best you're looking at is simple assault."

"This is what I recommend we do on the sentencing. A ten year prison sentence, and Steve gets credit for the time served so far. The balance of the sentence would be suspended, and Steve would be placed on five years probation. The terms of the probation would include completing the one year program at the halfway house in Millsville and an NA program in conjunction with that. We would also request work release and that Steve be allowed to possess an automobile at the center to get back and forth to work and counseling."

"Jon, you're really busting me on this one. Do you really want a repeat of the Rambler case? You thought for sure you had that in the bag, and you couldn't get a jury to convict a guy with ten ounces of meth in his pocket."

"This is completely different."

I was starting to get frustrated with Jon.

"Jon, think long and hard before this goes to trial. If you lose, you're just going to give Lacy Short ammo to crucify you. I really want to see you back in office after the election, I'm really just thinking about your future."

"Jackson, I can't do anything less than what I offered you."

"I'm under strict direction from my client not to accept any deal that involves prison time. Do you have any other offers?"

After a short pause, Jon said, "That's my final offer, Jackson."

"I'm sorry to hear that. I'll then have the clerk leave us on the docket for Monday then, and she can finalize the jury pool. I'll look forward to seeing you at trial."

"Thanks, Jackson."

"Thanks, Jon. I'll see you Monday."

The path for Steve Jones was beginning to have clarity. I walked to Jill's desk and said, "I need you to hold my calls for the rest of the week and make sure that my calendar is clear for the next two weeks. Jury selection for the Jones case starts on Monday."

"I'll take care of everything, Jackson."

"Thanks."

I walked back to my office and sat down. I had a few short days to finalize my case. I started by making a detailed list of exactly what needed to be done.

1. Closing Argument
2. Opening Statement
3. Final inventory of evidence
4. Subpoenas of all witnesses
5. Review the jury pool
6. Jury instructions
7. Talk to Steve

I decided to start at the bottom of the list. I grabbed my coat and headed to the jail to see Steve one last time before Monday morning.

Chapter XX

This was not just another Monday morning in Perkins County District Court. Today was the beginning of the trial of the decade. The two hours of sleep I was able to get last night would have to be enough. I'd worked through most of the night, trying to finalize the details of the case ahead of me. At about 4:00 a.m., I fell asleep at my desk. When my watch alarm went off at 6:00 a.m., I quickly got up and headed upstairs to clean up. I was very eager to get to Millsville to see Steve one last time before everything began. I took a quick shower and put on my favorite suit and the tie my mom had given me for law school graduation. I always felt confident wearing my black, double-breasted suit. It gave me the feeling that I was a knight about to head into battle and prepared for the weeks that lay ahead of me. I packed up my briefcase and headed to my garage. I decided to stop at the QuickStop on the way out of Renmus for a cup of coffee.

"Morning, Jackson."

"Hi, Stan. How are you today?"

"Not bad. So, word is today is a big day for you."

"You could say that."

"So, what's your prediction?"

"You know I don't pretend to know how these things will turn out.   Jon will present his case, I'll present mine, and the jury will decide what happens to Steve."

"You seem to be pretty calm. From what I've read in the paper, it looks like the state has solid case."

"You know better than to believe everything you read in the paper."

"Well, Jackson, it's hard not to believe it. The articles have been pretty clear about how Steve tried to kill his brother."

"I know they have. How much do I owe you?"

"Refills are only twenty-five cents."

I handed Stan my quarter and said good bye. He wished me good luck as I headed out of the store. I rolled out of the parking lot and onto the highway. I went through my opening statement in my head while I drove to Millsville. When I arrived, I could see that there was a lot of interest in the case. When I drove up to the front of the courthouse, I saw nearly fifteen news vans. I'd hoped to get into the jail to see Steve without being noticed but quickly realized that was going to be impossible. Being a creature of habit, I parked the Saturn about a block away from the courthouse. This gave me a little time for a quick walk and to get my blood moving. When I walked up the hill to the jail, the reporters noticed me and started yelling questions.

"Mr. Wright, do you think that your client is innocent?"

"Mr. Wright, who are your witnesses?"

"Mr. Wright, will you answer a few questions?"

I continued to walk, trying to pretend that I couldn't hear their questions.

"Mr. Wright, are there going to be any surprises in your case?"

This last question got my attention. I decided that it would be best to address the media briefly.

"I have time for a few questions."

I stopped and about ten reporters quickly gathered around me. Their camera people quickly turned on their equipment and gathered around.

"Mr. Wright, Chris Milton from KQRJ. What do you feel are the strengths of your case?"

"First of all, please feel free to call me Jackson. There's really no need for formalities with me. I'm going to do my best to present our case, and I'm sure Jon Hunlin will do a good job presenting the state's case. That's all we can do."

"We've heard that you believe that Mr. Jones is innocent."

I laughed and said, "It's not up to me to decide if he's guilty or innocent. That's up to the jury. I have time for one more question."

"Any predictions on the outcome?"

"No predictions. I'm confident about my case, and I'm going to do the best I can for my client."

A few more reporters continued to ask questions.

"I don't want to be rude, but I don't have time for any more questions. I need to talk to my client and get ready to select a jury today. I'll see all of you inside."

I turned and walked toward the sheriff's department. Once inside, I was greeted by the Sheriff.

"Crazy out there this morning."

"Sure is, Miles. Can you try to get a few of them to go easy on me?"

Miles laughed. "I'll do my best. Steve is waiting to talk to you. I'll take you in to see him."

"Thanks."

Steve was cleaned shaved and wearing a nice suit. It was shocking to see him all cleaned up. I'd only ever seen Steve in his orange, Perkins County jail attire. He was nervously walking back and forth in his cell. I stepped into the cell and sat down on the edge of the bed.

"How're you doing today, Steve?"

"I have to tell you, Jackson, I'm about ready to explode."

"Try to relax."

"I don't think I've been this nervous in my entire life."

"Look, Steve, I'm well prepared, and we have a pretty good case. This is going to be a long process, so try to get as much rest as you can."

"I'll try."

"There are a few things I want you to be aware of before we head over to the courthouse. First, when we are escorted out of the sheriff's department, there are going to be a lot of cameras and news people. I don't want you to answer any questions. I'll take care of that. Next, make sure that you keep yourself well-dressed and clean throughout the trial. Do you have any other suits?"

"Yeah. My mom brought me three."

"Good."

Steve kept pacing the cell and looking at the floor.

"One more thing. I want you to keep your head up. You need to look confident, and please, whatever happens in court, let me handle it. I don't want you to say a word."

"I promise I'll keep my cool."

"Good. Okay, are you ready?"

"As ready as I'm gonna be."

Miles escorted the two of us out of the sheriff's department, and the moment we emerged from the building, the cameras were quickly turned on. Steve appeared to be nervous and looked to me for reassurance.

"Keep your head up. We'll get through this."

Steve smiled, and we walked into the courthouse.

Chapter XXI

The Perkins County Courthouse was quite different from the other courthouses in the area. Recent renovations had modernized the entire building. The ceilings had been dropped and new sheetrock hung to make the courtroom seem quainter. The old courtroom had been divided into two smaller ones, and the only remaining sign of the historical, original courtroom were the pictures on the side wall of judges who had served in this room.

The benches were all modern, and the courtroom which once would have seated nearly two hundred, would be lucky now to seat twenty. The benches were nearly entirely full when I walked in with Steve. We approached the front of the courtroom and took a seat at the defense table. Jon Hunlin and one of his assistant county attorneys sat at the table to our left. Judy Joslin, Judge Quinn's court reporter, was seated in front of the bench to my left. The bailiff had seated himself behind the jury box also to my left, and Deputy Martin was sitting next to him. After about ten minutes the bailiff stood up and announced, "All rise. The Iowa District Court for Perkins County is now in session. The Honorable Thomas Quinn presiding."

Judge Quinn walked in and took his seat at the bench. He then spoke in his reserved voice, "Good morning, everyone. Please be seated."

As we all sat down, Judge Quinn continued. "This morning is an unusual morning in my courtroom. We have many members of the media present, so I feel that it's necessary to go over a few ground rules before we proceed. The parties have selected the jury in this matter, and we will be proceeding with the trial this morning. Before the jury is brought in, I would remind all of you that this is a court of law. I would ask that those present in the spectator gallery please remain silent at all times. If you are unable to that, I will have no choice but to clear the courtroom and prohibit spectators for the balance of the trial. I hope that I've made myself clear on this matter. Again, I welcome all of you here this morning."

Judge Quinn looked to his right and said, "Bailiff, will you please show in the jury."

Twelve people entered the courtroom from the jury room and entered the jury box. The group was comprised of four women and eight men. They ranged in ages from forty-three to sixty-seven. Once in the jury box, they all sat down. There were also twelve alternates selected, in case a juror were excused during the trial. The alternates took their place in the front two rows of the spectator gallery, which left about twelve seats for reporters and other spectators.

Judge Quinn looked at the jury and said, "Good morning. I would like to welcome all of you here today. Before we begin, I would like to remind the jury and all alternates that this case will be highly publicized. I would ask each of you not to communicate with any outside persons regarding this case while you are in the service of this court. Additionally, I would ask that all of you refrain from listening to or reading any news reports of this trial. Do any of you have any questions?"

The jury and alternates all shook their heads no.

"Hearing no questions, I would ask have you elected a foreman per my request?"

The gentleman sitting nearest to the judge stood and said, "Yes, your honor, I have been elected foreman of this jury."

"Good. You may be seated. All right, if the parties are ready, we can proceed."

Both Jon and I acknowledged that we were ready to begin, and Judge Quinn continued, "This is file number FECR52350, the State of Iowa v. Steven L. Jones. The charge against Mr. Jones is attempted murder. The parties presented to me, in chambers this morning, proposed jury instructions that they have agreed upon. I will review these instructions and address the parties about them on Friday. I believe that takes care of all the housekeeping matters for today. Mr. Hunlin, if you are ready to proceed, please go ahead with your opening statement."

Jon Hunlin stood up and walked toward the jury box. He stopped and looked at Steve for a split second and then turned his attention to the jury.

"Ladies and gentleman of the jury. You are going to see the evidence and hear witnesses' accounts of a horrific scene that took place in the quiet town of Hawkthorn. The eye witnesses will testify that they saw the defendant shoot not once, but three times at his brother Jeff. You will also hear testimony that, in his rage, the defendant stated numerous times that he was going to kill his brother. You will see the gun which the defendant used to shoot at his brother, and I will show you the bullets that were found at the scene. You will hear the testimony of the officers who investigated this crime and found that the defendant had, in fact, tried to murder his brother. When you have heard all of the testimony and seen all of the evidence, I am confident you will find beyond a reasonable doubt that Steve Jones attempted to murder his brother, Jeff. Thank you."

Jon walked back across the courtroom and sat down in his chair. I sat in my chair with my palms beginning to

sweat. My throat was dry, and my heart was racing. I heard
a voice from very far away and suddenly realized that it was
Judge Quinn saying that it was my turn to address the jury
with my opening statement. I took a deep breath and stood
up. At first, I thought that my legs were going to give out,
but I steadied myself with the help of the table and began to
walk toward the jury. "Good morning. I want to begin by
thanking all of you for being committed to finding the truth
in this case. I know that all of you have very busy lives, and
Mr. Jones and I appreciate the time that you are giving of
yourselves to serve on this jury. Ladies and gentlemen,
you'll be presented with a tremendous amount of
information over the course of this trial. The state will try to
convince you to believe a story that is simply not true. Your
job will be to figure that out. The evidence will show you
that none of the state's witnesses actually saw my client,
Steve Jones, fire a gun. Additionally, our own witnesses will
help you understand the true story of the events that
transpired. When the state is done presenting its case, Mr.
Hunlin will ask you to believe that Mr. Jones tried to murder
his only brother whom he deeply loved. You are going to
hear all kinds of tales and fantasy. I will show you that, in
fact, Mr. Jones had no reason to kill his brother and further,
that he never fired a single shot. In the end, after all the
evidence is presented, you will not be able to find beyond a
reasonable doubt that Steve Jones tried to murder his brother
or even fired a gun in Hawkthorn on March 1st of this year.
Mr. Jones and I thank you for listening closely to the facts.
Thank you."

As I turned to return to my seat, I paused and stared
at the reporters in the courtroom. I was still shocked to see
so many faces in the room. I was nervous about what they
would be reporting to the public. I took a few more steps,
picked up the pitcher from the table and poured myself a
glass of water. After I took my seat, I leaned over to Steve,

passed him a yellow note pad and pen, and wrote, "If you think of anything you think I should know during the trial, write it down. I'll be focusing on the witnesses and don't want to miss any testimony trying to answer a question for you, okay?"

"Yes."

I placed my arm on Steve's shoulder, trying to calm him and said, "I'm going to do my best for you."

He looked at me and smiled. His trial was now underway and the future of his life was in my hands.

Chapter XXI

"Mr. Hunlin, you may proceed."

"Thank you, your honor. The State calls Esther Smithers."

I watched Mrs. Smithers as she approached the witness box. She looked nervous. I speculated that this was probably the first time she had ever been in court. Judge Quinn greeted her and asked her to raise her right hand and to place her left hand on the bible that the bailiff was holding in front of her.

"Mrs. Smithers, do you swear to tell the truth, the whole truth and nothing but the truth?"

"I do."

"Please have a seat."

As Mrs. Smithers took her seat in the witness box, Jon Hunlin stood up. He started to walk to the center of the courtroom.

"Hello, Mrs. Smithers, I am Jon Hunlin. I am representing the State in a criminal matter against Steve Jones. Would you please state your entire name and address for the record?"

"You know my name and address, Jon."

Hunlin gave her a smile and said, "I know I do, Mrs. Smithers, but I need you to state it so that the court reporter can make it part of the record, please."

"Oh, I see. My name is Esther Marie Smithers, and I live at 55 West Pine Street in Hawkthorn."

"Thank you, Mrs. Smithers."

Mrs. Smithers nodded her head and smiled, "Certainly, Jon."

"Mrs. Smithers, Do you know who Steve Jones is?"

"I do."

"Is he present in court today?"

As she pointed to Steve, she said, "Yes, he is sitting over there."

"Can you tell me how you know Steve Jones?"

I stood up and said, "Objection, your honor. How she knows Steve Jones is not relevant to this case."

"Overruled. I want to see where this is headed for now. Mrs. Smithers you may answer the question."

I sat back down. I knew that Judge Quinn would allow the question, but I wanted to make an objection to help me relax and make sure that I was making a record in case I had to appeal the decision of the jury.

"I've known the Jones family for a long time. Steve lives with his mother and siblings across the town square from me."

"What can you tell me about Steve?"

"In my opinion, he's always been a trouble-maker. As long as I can remember, he's been causing problems. He used to ride his bike through my yard and throw rocks at cars as they drove by. He did all kinds of things that good little boys don't do."

I wished that I had objected to the question. I knew that the jury was getting a bad first impression of Steve.

"Did he stop doing those sort of things as he grew up?"

"Absolutely not! He and Jeff have bb gun fights and shoot bottle rockets at the kids in the neighborhood. I even saw them tip over the pop machine in the park to get free pop.

I can only imagine the things he did when no one was watching."

I felt at this point there was really no reason to object. Judge Quinn had let me know that he was going to allow this line of questioning. I sat back thinking of how I could offset these answers.

Jon continued pacing in the middle of the courtroom. "Do you remember March 1st of this year?"

"I sure do. It was a really cold day, and it was snowing. That was also the day that Steve Jones shot his brother."

I quickly rose from my seat, "Objection your honor, and I move to strike the second part of Mrs. Smithers' answer."

"Sustained." Judge Quinn looked over to the jury and said, "The jury will disregard the last portion of Mrs. Smithers' testimony." Judge Quinn then looked down at Mrs. Smithers and said, "Please, just answer the question that is asked. Do you understand?"

"I'm really sorry, you honor. I didn't know I wasn't supposed to say that."

I knew I needed to be very careful to protect my client with objections, while not appearing to be bullying Mrs. Smithers.

Hunlin continued, "Can you tell me what you remember seeing in the park on the afternoon of March 1st?"

"Well, to tell you the truth, I didn't see much at all."

"Just tell us what you remember."

"The first thing I remember was hearing a car come squealing around the corner and stop close by. I knew from the sound of the car that it was the Jones' car. The next thing I remember was hearing a lot of yelling and a big commotion, so I decided to go to the window and look outside to see what was going on."

"What did you see?"

"Well, the first thing I noticed was Jeff jumping over the bench and trying to crouch down. I didn't really think anything of that. I just figured he and Steve were up to their old stuff, but then, my gnome exploded."

"What happened to the gnome?"

I had to fight back my sudden urge to laugh at this question.

"Like I said, it exploded right in front of my eyes."

"Did you have any idea what made it do that?"

"Nope. But at that point, I knew the Jones' boys had had something to do with it, and I'd had enough."

"What did you do next?"

"I was upset about the gnome and thought that if I got the cops out there, they would make someone pay for my gnome. So I went over to the phone, and called 9-1-1. I told the dispatcher that there was a big commotion out in the park and that I thought it was a big fight with the Jones' kids."

"Do you remember what you did after that?"

"I waited inside my house, watching from my front window. I was anxious for the police to arrive."

"Did you notice anything else when you looked outside?"

"No."

"Thank you, Mrs. Smithers. I don't have any other questions for you."

"You're welcome, Jon."

Jon walked back to the prosecution table and sat down.

Judge Quinn then said, "Your witness Mr. Wright."

I stood up, walked around my table, and proceeded toward the jury box. "Thank you, your honor."

I stopped between the witness box and the jury box, as I alway did, forcing the witness to look at the jury when talking to me. I cleared my throat and said, "Good morning, Mrs. Smithers."

"Good morning, Jackson. It's good to see you again."

"It's nice to see you, too. Mrs. Smithers, I'm going to ask you a number of questions about the information you gave when Mr. Hunlin was asking you questions, okay?"

"Yes."

"Earlier, you said that you heard a car come squealing around the corner?"

"That's right."

"And then you said that you got up and walked over to your window to see what the commotion was?"

"I did."

"For the moment, I'd like you to just think only about the car, okay? Did you see anyone driving the car?"

"No. When I looked out the window the car was parked in front of the Jones' house. So I knew that one of those two boys had been driving it."

"You didn't see who was driving the car?"

"No."

"Were there any cars that were moving?"

"Yes. I saw one."

"Do you remember what that car looked like?"

"I think it was an Oldsmobile, but I couldn't tell you for sure. The car pulled up behind the Jones' car and parked."

"Did you see anyone get out of that car?"

"No."

"Could you see anyone sitting in that car?"

"Yes. I remember a young girl sitting in the car."

"March 1st was a pretty wild day, wasn't it?"

"It sure was, with my gnome and all."

"I want you to consider carefully about what you're about to say. Did you see anyone shooting?"

"No, I did not."

"Thank you, Mrs. Smithers. You have been very helpful. I have just a few more questions."

"That'll be fine."

"You know Jon Hunlin, personally. Is that correct?"

Jon quickly stood up, "Objection, your honor. Whether or not the witness knows me is irrelevant."

Judge Quinn looked as me and said, "Jackson?"

"Your honor, this line of questioning will go to the weight of Mrs. Smithers' testimony and her personal relationship with the prosecutor."

"I'm going to allow this line of questioning for now. Jackson, please try not to stray too far from your point."

"Certainly, your honor."

Jon sat back down and looked puzzled as to where I was headed with the question.

"Mrs. Smithers, let me repeat the question for you. Do you personally know Jon Hunlin?"

"I do. Jon's been my family's attorney for nearly thirty years and Jon's father was our attorney before that."

"So, he does your legal work?"

"He does. I really like him. He's such a nice man."

"You're aware that Jon is up for re-election this year, aren't you?"

Jon quickly objected, and Judge Quinn sustained the objection, warning me to watch where I was headed with my questions.

"I don't have any more questions for you, Mrs. Smithers. Thank you for being pleasant, as always."

"You're welcome, Jackson."

Judge Quinn looked down at Mrs. Smithers and said, "You can go, Mrs. Smithers. Thank you for your testimony."

Mrs. Smithers got up and walked out of the courtroom.

Judge Quinn looked down at his watch and said, "Why don't we go ahead and take a break for lunch at this time. I would ask the parties to please be ready to start this afternoon at 1:00 p.m."

Chapter XXIII

Just before 1:00 p.m., the parties filed back into the courtroom and assumed their respective positions at the counsel tables. The jury was shown in, and Judge Quinn welcomed everyone back.

"I hope that you all enjoyed your lunch. Mr. Hunlin, please call your next witness."

Jon rose and said, "Thank you, your honor. The state calls Stan Winfield."

Stan was a husky man. He stood nearly six feet three inches and appeared to weigh about two hundred fifty pounds. He reminded me of the television character Grizzly Adams. He had a full beard and long scraggily hair. He lumbered to the front of the courtroom. He was sworn in and took his seat in the witness box.

"Good afternoon, Mr. Winfield."

"Good afternoon."

Jon asked Stan questions about his background. Knowing that these formal questions would take a couple of minutes, I quickly thought back to my interview of Stan Winfield. He had surprised me when he stopped by my office shortly after noon on the 5th of July. He had not called for an appointment but had dropped by. I didn't find this to be that unusual because it was how most of my clients operated.

I knew I might not see Stan for another couple of months, so I set aside my lunch, and the two of us began to talk. He informed me that he hadn't seen Steve fire a gun, nor was he even quite sure who Steve was. I made sure to keep this information fresh in my mind as I refocused on Jon's questions.

"So, when did you first become aware of what was happening in the park?"

Stan, who had been staring at the pictures of the judges said, "Well, I was pretty focused on what I was doing. You see both Jason and I were under the hood of our new Freightliner, trying to figure out why it was running a little sluggish. I didn't even realize that anyone was in the park until Jason said, 'Did you hear that?' Then I said, 'Hear what?' Then he said, 'I think I heard a gun shot.' And I said, 'Are you sure?' So, both of us slid out from under the hood to take a look. That's when we noticed that the two Jones kids were having an argument."

"Did you see anything unusual?"

"The first thing I saw was some kid walking through the park pointing a gun at another guy. Then Jason just took off running at the kid with the gun. I figured I'd better go help him, 'cause I didn't want Jason getting shot."

"Do you remember what happened after that?"

"I saw Jason hit the kid with a wrench, but since I wasn't paying attention to where I was running, I tripped over the curb and fell. When I looked up, I saw the kid getting to his feet. The next thing I know the kid takes off running, but Jason couldn't go after him because he'd scrambled to get the gun. So I jumped to my feet and chased the kid down. I was afraid that the kid was going to get away."

"Did he?"

"Not a chance. I hit him so hard that I nearly knocked myself out. I don't think that I've hit anyone that hard since I hit Tommy Styles, the quarterback for Lingen, in the big game my senior year."

"What happened after that? Do you remember?"

"Well, it took me a couple seconds to shake off the haze. But then I saw the stupid kid getting to his feet. So I grabbed him by the back of the shirt and yanked him back to the ground."

"Did he put up much of a fight?"

"Yeah, that little guy is pretty quick. We wrestled for about five minutes. He nearly got away twice. He punched me in the face, and tried to kick me. He ended up biting me, so I flipped him onto his stomach and sat on his back. Once I got all my weight on him, I think he finally realized he wasn't going anywhere."

"So you sat on him?"

"That's right. I was able to get his arms pinned to his side by squeezing my legs tight against them. It was probably about another two or three minutes until the cops got there."

"Did anything happen while you were holding him down?"

"Not really. Once I got him under control, it was just a matter of waiting for the cops."

"Do you know Steve Jones?"

"Yes, he's sitting over there." Stan pointed to Steve.

"How do you know him?"

"Well, back in March, there was a shooting in the town square park in Hawkthorn, and Steve was arrested for the shooting. That's how I know who he is."

"So, just so I have your story straight. You and Jason Windsor were working on your semi. You heard Steve shooting and yelling at his brother."

Jon paused so I quickly stood up and said, "Your honor, I object. The county attorney is testifying, not asking a question."

"I'll sustain the objection. However, Jackson, I will remind you that you'll have an opportunity with this witness on cross-examination. I'm going to give the county attorney some latitude with his questions. Please rephrase the question."

I sat back down and Jon continued his question, "Thank you, your honor. Stan, you and Jason Windsor were working on your semi. While you were working on the semi, you heard a gun shot and yelling in the park?"

"That's correct. There were actually three gun shots."

"You, being a good citizen, hurried to the park to see if you could stop the shooter?"

"Yes."

"You had seen Steve Jones pointing a gun at another man across the park. Do you know who the other man was?"

"Yes, it was Jeff Jones, his brother."

"And finally, Jason was able to get the gun from Steve and you were able to hold Steve until the deputies arrived. Is that correct?"

"That sounds just like how I remember it happening."

Jon turned around, looked at me with a bit of a smirk, and then walked back to his chair. As he sat down, he said, "I have no further questions, your honor."

"Thank you, Mr. Hunlin. Mr. Wright, your witness."

I stood up, poured myself a glass of water, and said, "Thank you, your honor."

As I walked to my comfortable spot near the jury box, I asked, "Are you sure that the events in the park occurred exactly how you described?"

"Well, I'm pretty sure. It happened so long ago, I might have forgotten a thing or two."

"So, things might not have happened the way you just described them here in court under oath?"

"No, they did."

"I just want to be sure, because I wouldn't want you to get in trouble for not telling the truth."

I had Stan on the defensive, which was exactly where I wanted him.

"Stan, do you remember coming to my office to talk to me about this case?"

"I sure do. How could I forget your fancy office?"

"Thank you, Stan. Please try just to answer the questions I ask you and keep your commentary to yourself."

"Okay."

I was a bit anxious because Stan's testimony was different from what he had told me. Hunlin had obviously coached him on how to answer the questions. I now faced the challenge of getting the true version of Stan's story from him.

"You and Jason were working under the hood of your semi, correct?"

"Yes, that's correct."

"You said that you heard a gun shot and some yelling?"

"I did."

"You heard a gun shot?"

"Well, not exactly. Jason said he heard a shot, so I guess I just assumed that there was a gun shot."

"Okay, so you didn't hear a gun shot. Did you see anyone fire a shot?"

"Deputy Martin told me that Steve did."

"Again, did you see anyone fire a shot?"

"Well, no, I didn't see anyone shoot a gun."

"But yet you took off toward the park?"

"I did. When I saw Jason take off toward the park, I went to help him."

"Did you hear any other shots?"

"No. I was running, and I didn't really hear anything except some yelling."

"So, how do you know that shots were fired?"

"Deputy Kerns told me that Steve Jones had been firing shots at his brother Jeff."

"But you still think Steve was shooting at Jeff?"

"That's correct."

I looked over at the jury and could tell that they were interested that Stan hadn't seen Steve fire any shots, nor had he heard any shots.

"I see that you're wearing glasses. Can you tell me a little bit about your vision?"

"Yeah. I have to wear glasses. If I don't have my glasses on, the only things I can see more than a few feet away from me are fuzzy figures."

"Were you wearing your glasses the day in the park?"

"No, I'd put them on the bumper of the semi. I can see to work on the engine, and my glasses always fall down and get in the way. I had set them there so that they weren't getting in my way."

"Did you put them on before you took off for the park?"

"No."

"Had you ever seen Steve Jones or Jeff Jones before that day in the park?"

"No, I'd never seen either of them before."

"Do you remember going to the sheriff's department to identify Steve Jones?"

"I do."

"Were you able to identify him from a line up of five people?"

"I was not."

"So, how were you able to point out Steve Jones earlier?"

"Jason, Deputy Kerns, Deputy Martin, and Jon Hunlin have shown me a few pictures of the Jones brothers and told me that they were the people in the park. That is how I knew him."

"Stan, just so I am clear on everything. You didn't know Steve Jones; you didn't see him shooting; you didn't hear any gun shots; and you are only able to identify him now because of pictures you saw of him after the day in the park. Is that correct?"

"That's correct."

I walked back to my chair and sat down.

"I have nothing further, your honor."

Judge Quinn looked down at Stan and said, "Thank you, you're free to go."

Stan stepped down from the witness box and exited the courtroom.

Judge Quinn said, "Mr. Hunlin, looks to be about four o'clock. Will we be able to finish with another witness this afternoon?"

"No, your honor."

"Okay. I'm going to adjourn court for the day. But before the jury leaves, I need to remind all of you not to talk about this case with anyone. If you are questioned by the press, I would ask you please not to answer their questions. I would also ask that you please not read, watch, or listen to any news reports about this case. Do I make myself clear?"

All of the members of the jury acknowledged the judge.

"We will commence with the next witness at 9:00 a.m. sharp. Do the parties have anything else for the court?"

Jon and I both said that we did not.

"Okay, court is adjourned."

Chapter XXIV

Just as I had expected, Steve Jones was the lead story on every television station the area that night. I decided to watch part of the report on channel seven to get the feel for what was being presented to the public. I could only stand the first minute before I turned my television off in disgust. The morning's report wasn't mush better. When I stopped at the QuickStop to grab my coffee, Steve's name was plastered in bold print on the front page of the morning papers. Luckily, only Stan was in the store when I entered.

"Rough day yesterday?"

"It could have been worse."

Stan laughed. I dropped my quarter on the counter and headed on my way.

Again, the courthouse parking lot was filled with news vans and reporters. Not wanting to answer any questions this morning, I decided to pull around to the back of the courthouse and go in through the county recorder's office. Once I was inside, I took the back stairway to the second floor and entered the courtroom through the law library to avoid the media. I called the sheriff's department and asked Miles to bring Steve over to the courtroom. I sat down at my table, organized my notes, and prepared for day two. Jon was already fast at work when I arrived. He looked up and we exchanged pleasantries. Soon court would be back in session and I would be continuing to look for ways to protect Steve.

I glanced up when I heard the law library door open and saw Miles bringing Steve in. The two of them walked over to our table. Steve sat down, and Miles removed his handcuffs.

"Thanks for bringing him in the back way, Miles."

"No problem. I don't think that anyone should have to deal with this much media."

"Have a good day."

"You too."

Miles sat down on the bench directly behind me. I noticed that Beth had come to the trial today and that Marcella Jones, Steve's mom, was in the courtroom as well. A few minutes later, Judge Quinn entered and assumed his seat at the front of the courtroom. The jury was brought in and we were off to another day of testimony. Jason Windsor was on the witness stand and we were in full swing.

Jon had already run through the standard background questions and was moving into what Jason recalled from the shooting.

"Jason, can you please describe what you remember?"

"Well, things are a little fuzzy 'cause everything happened so fast, but I'll do my best. I was working on a semi with Stan Winfield. The next thing I know, I hear a loud pop. At first I thought that it was an M80 firecracker, but then I thought that it sounded more like a gun shot. So, I looked at Stan and said 'Did you hear that?'"

"What did Stan say?"

"He said, 'Hear what?' So I decided to look out from under the hood to see if I could see anything. I looked up and saw Steve practically running at Jeff with a gun. I knew right then that I'd heard a gun shot, so I took off to try to stop Steve. I've known him for a long time, so I figured I could probably calm him down."

"Do you remember how many gun shots you heard?"

"I only heard the one. After that, I was focused on getting to Steve as fast as I could and really just blocked out everything else. When I was running toward Steve, I yelled at him a couple of times, but he didn't look like he heard me. So when I got to him, I knocked the gun out of his hand and rushed over to pick it up. While I was getting the gun, Steve got to his feet in a hurry and took off. He didn't get far though because Stan was right behind me, and he tackled Steve. Stan was able to hold Steve until the cops showed up."

Jason's testimony didn't provide any surprises. Jon Hunlin's case was beginning to pick up steam, and thus far, Jason had been his best witness. I only had a few questions for Jason, and then he was dismissed. Jason had testified just as I had thought he would. I had kept a close eye on the expressions of the jury and believed that a few of them were beginning to have doubts as to the actual events that had occurred.

After the noon recess Hunlin called Deputy Kerns and Deputy Harms. The two of them described what they'd seen in the park and some of the information they'd gathered during the investigation. The afternoon was rather uneventful, but I knew that would soon change. The state had two more witnesses to present over the next two days, Deputy Martin and Jeff Jones, and I was excited to cross exam both of them.

Out in the parking lot, emotions were running higher than ever. Several deputies had been called out to settle down a number of protestors. It appeared that media had hit a nerve with a few people. I braced for the worst as I walked out of the courthouse. When I opened the door, there were at least fifty people holding signs and marching back and forth.

I heard one of the protestors yell, "Look, here comes that slimy attorney now!"

I fought back the urge to stop and introduce myself and proceeded to my car. I knew I needed to let yet another day of this trying time pass.

Chapter XXV

The final day of the first week was only going to be a half day. I was very excited to have the afternoon off, while Judge Quinn finalized the jury instructions. Tensions from the week were mounting, and I need some time to recover before things really heated up the next week. Fatigue is always a challenge, and I was struggling to make sure that I didn't drift this morning. Deputy Martin was an important witness, and I knew that if I could take a few cracks at his credibility, it would surely help me for the rest of the trial. Thus far, I'd been very impressed with Jon Hunlin. He had presented a strong case, and I was starting to have a few doubts about the strength of my own case. I had nearly fallen asleep waiting for Judge Quinn, but when I heard his voice, I was ready to go.

"Just a quick reminder, today we will only hear testimony in the morning. Then we'll enjoy the weekend and continue with things on Monday morning. With that being said, let's get started."

Deputy Martin was called to the stand and sworn in. I was glad to see that Jon had elected to remain seated to question this witness. A sure sign that he was tiring.

"How are you today, Deputy Martin?"

"I'm fine, Jon."

"Do you remember responding to a shooting in Hawkthorn on March 1st?"

"I do. The call came in around three p.m. Deputy Kerns, Deputy Harms, and I all responded to the call."

"Can you describe the scene when you arrived?"

"Yes. When I entered the park, I saw two individuals wrestling. I headed right for them, and hopped out of my cruiser. Deputies Harms and Kerns helped me secure the scene. We then arrested Steve Jones for the attempted murder of his brother."

"What did you do next?"

"Since Steve was being transported to the jail, I had time to investigate the crime scene for clues. I spent most of that evening inventorying the items we found and filling out reports."

"What sort of evidence did you find?"

"The first thing I did was take a look at the gun that Jason Windsor had taken from Steve. When I opened the pistol, I saw that there were three empty shell casings in the gun."

At that, Jon rose from his chair, picked up a clear baggy that contained three shell casings and a .22 caliber pistol, and walked toward Deputy Martin.

"Do you recognize the items in this bag?"

"I do. The casings are the ones I found in the gun, and the gun is the one that I secured at the scene."

"Your honor, I would like to introduce these items into evidence."

"Not hearing any objections, they will be accepted."

Jon returned to his table and sat back down.

"Did you find any other items?"

"Yes, I was able to locate the three discharged rounds."

"Where did you locate the rounds."

"The first one I located was in a piece of the gnome in Esther Smithers' yard. The second one was located in a piece of wood from a park bench. The final one was located in the grass behind the bench. This one had a piece of fabric on it that matched the fabric of the coat that Jeff Jones was wearing. I had ballistics tests run on all three of the bullets, and the results showed that they had been fired from a .22 caliber weapon."

"What type of gun did you seize at the scene?"

"It was a .22 caliber pistol."

"Which was the weapon that Steve Jones had been in possession of?"

"That is correct."

"Nothing further, your honor."

I stepped around the defense table and for a change of scenery stepped to the middle of the courtroom.

"Good afternoon, Deputy Martin."

"Afternoon, Jackson."

"I just have a couple of questions for you. First, did the ballistics test show a match between the shots fired and the gun you found?"

"The ballistics tests indicated that the bullets were fired from a .22 caliber weapon."

"So, the tests did not verify the weapon you seized as the only possible weapon?"

"No, I guess it's possible there could have been another weapon."

"Did you look for any other weapons?"

"No. We had no reason to believe that there were any other weapons."

"So, it's possible that another weapon could have fired the shots."

"Possible, but highly unlikely. This gun had three empty casings, the exact number of shots that were said to have been fired, and we located all three of the shots."

"Who did you interview as potential witnesses?"

"We interviewed everyone in the neighborhood to see if they had seen anything and the people that were at the scene when we arrived."

"Did you interview Beth Zable?"

"Yes. She came into the office and told us her story. I didn't think that her story held water."

"Did you interview Samuel Baxter?"

"No, we talked to his parents, and they said nobody in their family saw anything."

"Thank you, I don't have any further questions."

Deputy Martin left the courtroom, and I returned to my seat. Court was adjourned for the day, and we all left the courthouse. I left thinking about the upcoming testimony of Jeff Jones and of my own witnesses. The trial was passing by quickly, and Steve Jones' fate would soon be decided. It was a relief to finally take a break.

Chapter XXVI

Jeff was the state's key witness, and I knew that I need to be well-prepared. Monday would potentially be the hardest day of the trial. Jeff Jones could identify Steve, and he was still bitter about being in the McKee Center for his possession conviction. On my way home Friday afternoon, I thought about his sentencing in Stoker County. I had been in the back of the courtroom waiting for a sentencing hearing for one of my clients and was able to witness first hand his fate for admitting that the marijuana in the Charger was his. Lacy Short represented him, and I found it enjoyable just to sit back and watch for a change. Judge Wilson presided over the sentencing, and I knew things might not go well for Jeff.

"It is my understanding that the State is going to amend its charges against Mr. Jeff Jones and that the parties have agreed on a plea agreement in this matter. Is that correct Mr. Williams?"

"Yes, your honor. As part of a plea agreement, the State in this case has agreed to amend the charges to possession of marijuana, second offense, an aggravated misdemeanor, from the charge of possession of marijuana, third offense, a class D felony."

"Is that correct, Ms. Short?"

"Yes, your honor."

"Before I accept your plea of guilty to the amended charges, Mr. Jones, it is necessary for me to ask you a few questions. Do you understand?"

"Yes, your honor."

Jeff showed the same respect to Judge Wilson that Steve had shown to me.

"First of all, Mr. Jones, has your attorney, Ms. Short, explained to you the amended charge and the potential penalties that can be imposed against you for that charge?"

"Yes, sir."

"Has your attorney discussed with you what the State's recommendation for your sentence would be should you wish to plead guilty to that charge today?"

"Yes."

"Has anyone threatened you in anyway to force you to enter a plea of guilty to the charge of possession of marijuana, second offense?"

"No, your honor."

"Are you doing so of your own free will?"

"Yes, your honor."

"Do you understand that by entering a plea of guilty today to these charges that you are giving up your constitutional right to a speedy and public trial, to question witnesses the state may bring against you, and to present evidence on your own behalf?"

"I do, your honor."

"Do you also understand that if you enter a plea of guilty today, that at no time in the future will there be a trial on this matter and you can never appeal your plea of guilty on those grounds?"

"I do."

"Has a plea agreement been presented to you in this matter?"

"Yes, one has."

"Do you understand that the court is not bound to follow the sentencing agreement and can enter any sentence the court deems appropriate up to and including the maximum sentence of 2 years in the Iowa State Correctional Facility and a $5,000 fine?"

"Yes, your honor."

"Did your attorney, Ms. Short, go over that with you?"

"She did, your honor."

"Knowing this, do you still wish to enter a plea of guilty to the charge of possession of marijuana, second offense an aggregated misdemeanor?"

"I do, your honor."

"Mr. Jones, I then ask you: how do you wish to plead to the amended charge of possession of marijuana, second offense?"

"Guilty, your honor."

"The court finds your plea of guilty to be of your own free will, that you do so knowingly and will accept your plea of guilty to this charge."

Judge Wilson looked down at the courtroom and took a deep sigh.

"Do the parties wish to proceed to sentencing today?"

Both Thompson Williams and Lacy Short acknowledged that they did, so Judge Wilson continued to question Jeff.

"Mr. Jones, do you understand that you do not need to proceed to sentencing today? That you can have your sentencing set for a later date, and you can call witnesses on your behalf to present evidence regarding sentencing?"

"I do, your honor."

"Knowing this, do you wish to delay your sentencing in order to prepare or do you wish to proceed with sentencing today?"

"I wish to go to sentencing today."

"Will the State please present the agreement of the parties?"

Thompson Williams stood behind his table and addressed the judge.

"Your honor, the parties have agreed that in exchange for Mr. Jones' plea of guilty to the amended charge of possession of marijuana, second offense, the State will recommend the following sentence. First of all, that Mr. Jones be sentenced to two years in the Iowa State Correctional Facility, but that the entire sentence be suspended except for the 3 days Mr. Jones has served in the Stoker County jail and that he be given credit for time served on those days. Secondly that Mr. Jones be placed on two years probation with the Iowa Department of Corrections, that the terms of his probation require that he be placed in the McKee Center for rehabilitation, and that that he complete a narcotics treatment program while at the McKee Center."

"Is that the entire agreement of the parties, Mr. Williams?"

"Yes, your honor."

"Is that your understanding of the agreement, Ms. Short?"

"Yes, your honor. However, Mr. Williams forgot to include that he would not object to Mr. Jones being granted work release from the McKee Center since he has incurred a fair amount of fines and debt related to this case."

"Is this true, Mr. Williams?"

"Yes, your honor. My mistake. The State does not object to a request for work release."

"Is there anything else that either of the parties believes is relevant before I enter a ruling in this matter?"

Jon said, "No, your honor."

Judge Wilson looked over at Lacy Short, and she stood to address him.

"Your honor, I would like to say a few words on Jeff's behalf."

"Go ahead, Ms. Short."

"Your honor, Mr. Jones made a few mistakes on the day he committed this crime. He is acknowledging here in open court that he committed the crime and is prepared to serve any sentence that you decide to impose on him. He has been an active member of the Methodist Church here in town and was employed at the Conoco Station before his arrest. I have talked to his supervisor at Conoco, and I have a letter from him acknowledging that, if Mr. Jones is granted work release, he will be allowed to continue his employment there. It is my belief that Mr. Jones understands the severity of his actions. We respectfully request that you follow the recommendations of the State and enter an order sentencing him to those recommendations. Thank you, your honor."

"Thank you, Ms. Short. Mr. Jones, will you please rise so that I can enter a sentence."

Jeff rose and stood next to Lacy.

"Mr. Jones. I believe that the crime you committed in this case was egregious. You appear to be remorseful, but I'm not sure whether you're sorry for what you did or just sorry that you got caught."

"I believe that the state's recommendation for this crime is very lenient and I have entered much harsher penalties for lesser crimes."

Jeff was now visibly shaken.

"However, since the parties have reached an agreement as to sentencing, and because you came forward and cleared your brother of this crime, I will impose the sentence, as recommended."

Jeff sighed with relief. It appeared to me that he had been holding his breath for the entire time that Judge Wilson had been speaking.

"The court hereby orders that you shall be sentenced to five years in the Iowa State Correctional Facility, that you be given credit for the 3 days you have served here in the Perkins County jail, that the balance of your sentence will be suspended and that you serve a term of probation that will last two years. The terms of that probation will place you in the McKee Center until you complete that program. While you are in the McKee Center, you will have work release privileges and you will be required to complete a Narcotics Anonymous program."

Great relief was evident on Jeff's face.

"Do the parties have anything else for the court?"

Both Thompson and Lacy stated that they did not.

"Ok, then, court is adjourned."

Chapter XXVII

The McKee Center was named after the late state representative who had been an advocate for drug rehabilitation, and Jeff had been there for two days. The closest NA program was located in Jensen, a town of about ten thousand people, fifteen miles from the Center. For the most part, Jeff was free to come and go from the McKee, as long as he was going to an appointment or work. Jeff could check himself out of the facility to do some shopping and run errands. All in all, it was a pretty sweet deal Lacy Short had gotten for him, considering that Jeff had been convicted of possession of marijuana three times.

At about five thirty in the afternoon, the Friday before Jeff was to testify, he checked out of the McKee Center to go to his first NA meeting in Jensen. On his way, he decided to stop at Star Meslin's house. Star had recently moved from Lingen to Jensen, and she was sitting on her front porch when Jeff pulled up in the Charger.

"Hey, Star, how've you been?"

"What are you doing here, Jeff?"

"I have to go to an NA meeting over at the Catholic Church. Just thought that I'd stop by and say hello. I've really missed you."

"What time does your meeting start?"

"Six, I've got sometime to waste until I've to be there."

"Would you like to come in for a little bit?"

She reached out, pulled Jeff close, and gave him a big hug. Jeff looked down at her and kissed her on top of her head. Then, he picked Star up and carried her into her living room. She was smiling and giggling as he placed her on the couch, and the two of them continued to hold and kiss each other. Star placed her hand on Jeff's leg and began to massage it. He was starting to feel the urge to kiss her entire body.

"Do you like that?" Star whispered in Jeff's ear.

"I do, but I can't. I really just need someone to talk to."

She started to kiss his neck, and Jeff did nothing to stop her. He was enjoying the female companionship and was in no hurry to get to the NA meeting. Star unbuttoned Jeff's pants and slid her hand inside his jeans and down his leg, continuing her soft caress. Jeff jumped up.

"I can't, Star. Can we just talk for a few minutes?"

Star looked up at Jeff.

"I'm sorry. I've just been lonely."

"I need to talk about Steve. I'm supposed to testify at his trial on Monday. I'm really nervous about it. I don't want him to get into any more trouble."

"What are you going to do?"

"I don't know yet. I've been running all kinds of ideas through my head and trying to figure it all out. I know that the State's case will be really weak if I don't testify and that would help Steve. I know he'd do anything for me, and I just want to help him."

"It's okay to be nervous. Your brother means a lot to you, and you don't want him to go to prison. But you have to remember you're already in a lot of trouble, and you don't need to make that any worse."

"That's true. I just wish I could run away."

"I know. Life is hard sometimes. Can you stay a little longer? I'll make us something to eat."

"No, I should probably get going."

"To your meeting?"

"Yeah, but I don't think I'm going to go."

"What? Why not? You know that they check on those things."

"I know, but I don't think I can handle being locked up anymore, and I'm really freaked out about testifying against Steve. I've had enough of this whole thing and just want it to go away."

"Jeff, you can't do something stupid."

"Why don't we go to Canada?"

"What?"

"Well, I've been thinking of taking off, and it would be nice to have some company. Come with me, Star!"

"Jeff, you know I can't do that. You're just thinking crazy."

Star was starting to be very nervous. She knew that Jeff was very persistent and could be very forceful in getting what he wanted. She did not want to cross him, but she had no interest in running away to Canada with him either.

"Why not? It'll be fun."

"You need to go to your meeting, Jeff."

"No, I don't. They're just going to tell me not to do drugs. I already know everything about that."

"But you'll get in trouble," Star pleaded.

"Yeah, maybe. But it's not like I haven't gotten in trouble before."

Jeff walked across the living room to the front door. When he got to the door, he stopped, reached down, and gave Star a kiss and a hug.

"Please, don't do this Jeff."

"Sorry, I'm going."

"Jeff, please."

Jeff started heading down the sidewalk to the Charger that was sitting at the curb. Star yelled after him.

"Come back soon, Jeff."

"Star, you know that you've always been special to me."

"Jeff, I love you," Star yelled after him

Jeff waved goodbye and hopped into the front seat of the Charger. Instead of turning the car around and heading back into Jensen, he kept the car pointed north and headed out of town. Star sat for a minute, wondering what the hell Jeff was doing. She didn't move for nearly five minutes, hoping that Jeff would come back by her house and head back into Jensen to the Catholic Church for his meeting. But Jeff was nowhere to be seen. Knowing what Jeff might be up to, Star started to feel a bit uneasy, especially since she'd been the last person to see Jeff in Jensen. She knew that if Jeff didn't go to his meeting and the McKee Center found out, she might get in trouble for being seen with him before he left town.

At ten after six, when Jeff still hadn't come back to Jensen, she walked inside her house and sat on the floor in front of her telephone. Thinking hard about what might happen to Jeff if she called the police and thinking hard about what might happen to her if she didn't, Star finally picked up the phone and dialed 9-1-1.

"This is the Minster County dispatcher. What is the nature of your emergency?"

Star sat quietly, not knowing what to do or say. The voice on the phone spoke again with a little more urgency.

"What is your name?"

Star began to speak slowly and nervously.

"Star Meslin."

"What is your emergency, Star?"

"I just had a friend stop by my house."

"Ok, Star. What happened?"

After a long pause, the voice spoke to her again.

"What is your friend's name, Star?"

"Jeff Jones."

"What did Jeff do, Star?"

Star, not able to speak, sat clutching the phone in her hand and pressing it hard to her ear.

"Star, we can't help you unless you talk to me. Did Jeff hurt you?"

"No."

More silence on the phone. The dispatcher spoke again.

"What did Jeff do, Star?"

"He's running from the cops."

"I need to know which way he's headed Star."

"I think north."

"Do you know what he is driving, Star?"

Star didn't respond.

"I need to know what he's driving, Star. Nothing is going to happen to you. Please just tell me what he's driving."

"His Charger."

Star dropped the phone, fell over onto her stomach, and started to cry. She knew what she'd done and why she'd done it, but it still didn't make her feel any better. Star had been in love with Jeff since they were in eighth grade, she had dated Steve to get closer to Jeff, and she didn't want to hurt him. She knew that Jeff was going to be in a lot of trouble and that she would be the one who had ratted him out. She continued to cry on the floor and the voice in the phone seemed a million miles away.

"Star. Stay with me Star. Star!"

Star hung up the phone and lay motionless on the floor, crying.

The dispatcher had activated an emergency call to the Minster County Sheriff's Department and had also made an emergency call to the Rath County Sheriff's Department, one county north of Minster. Deputies from both counties were quickly put on the lookout for Steve. The dispatcher had run a search and found that Jeff owned a 1974 Charger.

About twenty minutes later, the Charger was spotted by Deputy Waters in Rath County. The deputy tried to close position without being seen by Jeff. Just then a second Deputy, Deputy Patrick, coming from the northern part of Rath County, passed Jeff on the highway. Steve and Deputy Patrick made eye contact, and Jeff knew right away that they were looking for him. He hit the gas, and the engine of the Charger roared. Deputy Patrick whipped a u-turn right in front of Deputy Waters, who had to swerve to miss him. Both deputies hit their lights and raced down the highway after Jeff. Jeff had a head start, but he knew that the cops had radios and that his only hope was to try to lose them and ditch the Charger.

After about three miles, the deputies had closed the distance between them and Jeff to about five feet. Deputy Patrick bumped the back of the Charger since Jeff had shown no sign of giving up. Jeff looked in the rear view mirror and flipped Deputy Patrick the bird. Deputy Waters was trying to position himself to the left of Charger, but as they started up a steep hill at full speed, Deputy Waters decided to drop back in line. Deputy Patrick again struck the back of the charger and this time, forced Jeff to hit the gravel on the right side shoulder.

Jeff swerved back onto the road and again looked in his rear view mirror and shouted.

"*KNOCK IT OFF!*"

As they cleared the hill, nothing but flat road lay ahead of them for nearly two miles. Deputy Waters again pulled along side of the Charger, while Deputy Patrick flanked the car from behind. This time Deputy Waters initiated the contact on the Charger and forced it into a ditch. Jeff hadn't been wearing his seatbelt and was thrown from the vehicle as it rolled end over end five times before coming to rest on its hood in a nearby field. Jeff lay motionless on the ground as both of the deputies rushed toward him.

Suddenly, Jeff jumped to his feet, pulled out a pistol, and headed for the cornfield. Deputy Patrick and Deputy Waters raised their own firearms and gave chase.

Deputy Patrick yelled, "Drop the gun!"

Jeff stopped for a split second, turned back to the officers, and fired a shot in their direction. Both of the deputies dropped to the ground and hid behind the edge of the ditch. They both returned fire, and their shots whizzed into the cornfield behind Jeff. Jeff started to laugh and fired two more shots at the deputies. The second one hit Deputy Waters square in the left arm. He fell backwards and rolled to the bottom of the ditch. Blood was running down his arm and the pain from the bullet started to radiate toward his fingers.

Jeff started to climb through the barbed wire fence at the edge of the cornfield. Deputy Patrick took aim and fired again, this time hitting Jeff in the left leg, and Jeff fell back toward the deputies. As Jeff rolled from his back to his stomach, Deputy Patrick was rushed toward him, trying to get to Jeff before he could fire again. In the meantime, Deputy Waters had made his way back to the top of the ditch and was about thirty feet behind Deputy Patrick and taking aim at Jeff. Jeff made it to his knees and raised his gun at Deputy Patrick.

From behind him, Deputy Patrick heard Deputy Waters shout, "Drop the gun!"

In response, Jeff pointed the gun directly at Deputy Patrick. Both deputies could see the grin on Jeff's face and could tell that he looked very controlled as he attempted to steady the gun. Deputy Patrick had closed to six feet away from Jeff, but had stopped dead in his tracks. Deputy Patrick started to think about his wife and kids for the first time, thought that he might never see them again.

Jeff slowly said, "I'm not going back."

As Jeff moved to pull the trigger, Deputy Waters fired from behind Deputy Patrick and hit Jeff square in the chest. Jeff was propelled backwards from the shot and lay motionless on his back. His gun had fallen to the ground, and Deputy Patrick quickly seized it.

Jeff lay on the ground, looking up at the blue sky, and enjoyed a moment of peace until both deputies were standing over him with their guns drawn. He knew with perfect clarity that he was soon going to die.

Jeff looked up at the deputies as he gasped for air, smiled at both of them, and then said. "Wasn't that fun?"

The two deputies looked at each other with relief. Deputy Patrick called the dispatcher and told her that they'd caught Jeff Jones just short of the state line.

"We need two ambulances as soon as possible. Deputy Waters has been shot and so has Jeff Jones."

"Is everyone all right?"

"Just get the ambulances here as fast as possible."

Deputy Waters sank down to the ground and applied pressure to his arm, trying to stop the bleeding. Deputy Patrick rushed back from his cruiser to try to stop the bleeding from Jeff's chest.

"Stay with us, Jeff. The ambulance is on its way."

Jeff lay on the ground in a pool of his own blood, not saying a word. He thought back to the times he'd spent with his brother, growing up in this rural part of Iowa. His breaths had become shorter and he could taste blood with each breath. In the distance, he could hear the sound of approaching sirens, but he knew that the ambulance was going to be too late. Jeff grabbed Deputy Patrick by the arm

and squeezed as hard as he could. It was only a matter of
seconds before he released his grip, his arm falling lifelessly
to the cool Iowa farm ground where his dead body now lay.

Chapter XXVIII

Around four thirty Friday afternoon, Spencer and I packed up the Jeep and finished getting ready to head for the river. I was feeling very relaxed having, the afternoon off from the Jones' trial. The only thing on my mind was enjoying the company of a couple friends and water skiing for an hour or two.

"Where's Lynn?"

"She decided to drive the Jetta. She left with the dogs about twenty minutes ago."

"So we're meeting her in Lansing?"

"Yeah. Can you do me a favor? Run over to the grocery store and grab a couple of bags of ice while I arrange the rest of the stuff."

"No problem."

I headed for Christopherson's Family Foods, the only grocery store in town. There were only two choices when it came to buying groceries in Renmus. One could pay the inflated prices at Christopherson's or drive thirty minutes to Waterloo. Wanting to support another local business, I usually purchased my groceries at Christopherson's. As I entered the grocery store, I ran into Chuck Walsh, a local banker.

"Hi, Chuck."

"Jackson, I hear you've been giving Hunlin the once over in that Jones trial."

"Well, Judge Quinn is an honorable man. He's holding a fine proceeding."

"Any other interesting cases brewing for you?"

"You know I can't talk about my other cases."

"Thought I'd see if you'd tell me. You know you can trust me. By the way, why aren't you in court?"

"Judge Quinn gave all of us the afternoon off, so Spencer and I are heading up to the river."

"Going to get in some skiing?"

"Yeah, first day I've been able to get away in a long time."

"Well you have fun. It's good to see you."

"You too, Chuck."

I walked to the opposite side of the store. Christopherson's had five aisles. The selection was limited, but they had the essentials. I grabbed the ice and headed to the checkout stand. Marge Simms, Jarvis Simms' wife, was the checkout attendant. I stepped up to her cash register with my two bags of ice.

"Afternoon, Marge. How's Jarvis?"

"Hello, Jackson. He's fine. Heard about what you're doing for the Jones kid. I think you should be ashamed of yourself."

I looked down at the bags of ice and then back at Marge. I felt uneasy even though I'd known that conversations like this were bound to happen.

"I'm just doing my job, Marge."

"People like my husband work hard to make sure people like Steve Jones go to jail, and people like you come around and get them out on a technicality."

Trying to change the subject, I asked Marge how much I owed. She told me I owed three dollars and thirty-seven cents, so I handed her the money and said good bye as

I picked up my ice and walked out of the store. When I got back across the street to where Spencer was waiting for me, I handed the ice to him.

"Do we need anything else?"

"I think that will do it. Will you grab the other side of the cooler?"

We lifted the cooler into the back of the Jeep, and then hopped in. Spencer hit the gas, and we headed east out of Renmus. Neither of us said much for the first twenty minutes of the drive. Then I looked to the south and the sky was looking very black. It appeared that a summer storm was developing around us.

"Spencer, look at that."

Spencer looked to the south in the direction I was pointing.

"Looks like we might get a storm."

"Figures, the one day that I can get out of the office and it storms."

"We should probably stop in Jensen and put the top up."

"Sounds good."

We kept driving toward the river, and the sky kept getting darker. When we pulled into a convenience store in Jensen to put the top on the Jeep, we could hear thunder and the lightning strikes hit one after another. The two of us hurried to get the top up so we would stay dry. As we finished, three bolts of lightning lit up the western sky and darkness was starting to set in.

"Looks like this is going to be a pretty good storm."

"Yeah, I'm going to give Lynn a call and let her know that a storm is coming her way. I'll ask her to head up to Bizarre's Pizza and order dinner."

Spencer walked away from the Jeep, trying to find better reception for his cell phone. He spent about two minutes talking to Lynn and then hopped into the driver's seat of the Jeep. A light rain had started, but we could tell that much heavier precipitation was on the way. We knew we wanted to get back on the road and ahead of the storm if we could.

"All right. We're all set. Lynn is going to order pizza, and we should be eating dinner and enjoying a beer in about twenty-five minutes."

We pulled out of the parking lot and back onto the highway. The storm was still gaining on us, and the rain was beginning to fall much heavier. The windshield wipers were having a heck of a time keeping the windshield clear. We drove for about twenty minutes, which normally would've put us in Lansing, but with the rain, we still had about five miles to go.

"Hell of a storm."

"Sure is. Gotta' love Iowa weather."

A flash of lightning streaked the sky and a sharp crash of thunder exploded, just as my cell phone rang.

I looked at Spencer, and said, "That was creepy."

He just laughed.

"This is Jackson."

"Hi, Jackson. It's Joan, Judge Quinn's court clerk. Sorry to bother you after hours."

"No worries. What's up?"

"Something has happened to Jeff Jones. Judge Quinn would like you to call him at home."

I was silent for a moment and began to feel uneasy.

"Did he say what it was about?"

"No, just that it was urgent for you to call."

"That's no good. Okay. Thanks, Joan. I'll give him a call right away."

Spencer looked at me and asked if everything was okay. I said that I needed to make a call. Something had happened to Jeff Jones. We were finally in Lansing, and we both jumped out of the Jeep and ran into Bizarre's.

"Hi, Lynn."

Lynn was sitting at the table just inside the door.

"Hi, guys."

I looked at Spencer and Lynn and told them I'd be right back. I walked to the other side of the building where it was quiet and there were no patrons. I dialed Judge Quinn's home number and sat down.

"Judge Quinn."

"Hi, Judge. This is Jackson Wright."

"Hi, Jackson. Thanks for calling me back so quickly. Enjoying your day away from trial?"

"Sure, I'm up at the Mississippi River, enjoying the break. We're hoping to go skiing as soon as the storm passes."

"Well, Jackson. I have a bit of news to pass along."

"What do you mean, Judge?"

My nervousness was beginning to be confirmed.

"Early this afternoon, Jeff Jones was killed."

I stood up and began to pace frantically.

"What? How? Where?"

"Slow down, Jackson. Just relax."

"Sorry, your honor. What happened?"

I had walked almost to where Spencer and Lynn were sitting and back.

"Well, he took off from the McKee Center earlier. Jeff got into a high speed chase with deputies in Rath County. The deputies were able to run him off the road, but once they got Jeff stopped, he started shooting at them. The officers returned fire, and one of the shots hit Jeff in the chest. He died from that shot."

I sat down in disbelief.

"I don't know what to say."

"Jackson, I'm going to continue the trial until Tuesday."

"Okay. Thanks, your honor."

"If you need anything, let me know."

"I will."

I hung up my cell phone and placed it on the table were I was sitting. I picked up the beer that Spencer had brought me and chugged it. Then, I walked to the bar and asked the bartender to bring me a shot of tequila and sat down with Spencer and Lynn. Lynn looked at me with concern and asked if everything were okay. I didn't say anything for a couple of minutes and just sat there waiting for the bartender. He finally brought my shot of tequila and placed it in front of me. I picked up the glass and held it for a second. I studied the shot over and over and Lynn continued to ask what was wrong. I finally drank the shot, slammed the glass back onto the table and said, "Jeff Jones is dead."

Chapter XXIX

I used the extended weekend to finalize the evidence I was going to present. I used Monday to review the testimony of the State's witnesses and to figure out exactly how to counter the statements of each witness. I arrived early at the courthouse on Tuesday, as usual, I spent a few minutes trying to comfort Steve. He looked very upset and unable to focus on his own problems.

Judge Quinn entered the courtroom and took his seat on the bench. He looked as if he'd had rough weekend.

"I'd like to welcome everyone back. I want to extend my sympathy to Steve Jones and his family for the loss of Jeff Jones. I apologize about the delay in the trial, however I felt that it was necessary to allow everyone an extra day to regroup. I'm going to tend to a few housekeeping issues before we get started. I received the jury instructions that were proposed by the parties early last week. I reviewed them on Friday afternoon and find them to be acceptable. I will also ask that each of the news stations refrain from further video in the courtroom. I think that's everything I have. Do the parties wish to address any other matters before I have the jury brought in?"

Hunlin stood, "Your honor, I would ask to continue this matter for one week. I'd like to be able to review this matter and attempt to settle the case in light of the recent events."

"Jackson?"

"Your honor, I've had time to review in preparation for trial, and I'm ready to proceed. If Jon wishes to discuss resolving this case without continuing the trial, I'm available to do so after the testimony this morning. It's my personal opinion that it's in the best interests of fairness to continue with the trial today."

"I'm going to deny the State's request for a continuance. Jon, if you wish to discuss a settlement with Jackson, you do so after court today. Anything else?"

Jon sat back down, and I stood up.

"Your honor, I don't know if we can do anything about the cameras and protesters immediately outside the courthouse, but it's getting harder each day to get into the courthouse and it's putting additional strain on my client. Would you consider making an order requiring the cameras and protesters to stay at least fifty feet from any courthouse entrance?"

"I understand your concern, Jackson, but I'm going to deny your request. I know that it's a hassle, but it's one we can all live with for just a little longer. Okay, let's get to it. Bailiff, please show the jury in."

The jury was escorted in, and as they assumed their seats in the jury box, they looked tired and ready for this matter to be wrapped up. I was glad that the jurors had not been in the room when the death of Jeff had been discussed. I knew that most of the them would have heard the news but believed that it was good that they hadn't heard it here.

"Mr. Hunlin, does the State wish to present any further evidence?"

"Your honor, at this time the State rests its case."

"Mr. Wright, the defense may proceed."

"Thank you, your honor. The Defense calls Beth Zable."

Chatter started in the back of the courtroom. Judge Quinn quickly slammed his gavel down and said in a strong voice, "I would remind the spectators in the court to remain quiet. If you can't do that, I will clear the court room."

The spectators continued to discuss my first witness in a hushed whisper. Beth walked to the front of the courtroom and took her place in the witness box. The jury was studying her very closely. When cross-examining Deputy Martin, I had hinted that she had knowledge that the State had not pursued. I quickly stood up and greeted Beth.

"Good morning, Beth."

She smiled and said, "Hello."

"Could you please describe for the jury your relationship with Steve Jones?"

"Steve and I have been going out for about a year. He's been in jail for half that time, but I love him and would do anything for him. He's always treated me well and has taught me so many things about myself. I was really bummed that he couldn't take me to the prom or be at my graduation, but I'm hoping that he'll be home soon so our relationship will continue to grow."

"Are you currently in college?"

"No, I decided that the stress from this trial was too much to start school this fall. I'm going to wait and start college in January."

"Do you know everyone in the Jones family?"

"I sure do," she said with a smirk. "Marcella and her two girls are wonderful, but Steve's brother Jeff was something else."

"Why do you say that?"

"Steve worshiped Jeff, and Jeff used to take advantage of that. He slept with Star Meslin, behind Steve's back, and everyone in the entire area knew that except for

Steve. He encouraged Steve to get into fights and to do all kinds of juvenile pranks. Most of Steve's problems were caused by Jeff."

"And Steve would do these things?"

"Steve wanted his brother to be proud of him."

"Can you describe Steve for me?"

Beth was painting the exact picture of Steve and Jeff's relationship that I had wanted. The jury was very in tune to what Beth was saying and I could see that many of them were beginning to believe that Steve might not have shot at his brother.

"Would you lie to protect Steve?"

"No, I wouldn't. My parents taught me to always tell the truth."

"Do you remember what happened in Hawthorn on March 1st?"

Hunlin sprung to his feet, "Objection your honor. This is hearsay. She has no actual knowledge of what happened in the park."

"Jackson?"

"Your honor, I believe it will be apparent that it's not hearsay."

"I'm going to sustain the objection. Jackson, if you wish to proceed this way, I'd recommend you lay some foundation as to her knowledge of the events."

Jon was settling back into his chair.

"Beth, can you tell about what happened between you and Steve the afternoon of March 1st?"

Jon was on his feet again, "Objection your honor, what happened with her isn't relevant."

"Your honor, if you allow me I'll show the relevance."

"Overruled. You may proceed."

"Thank you. Again, Beth can you tell me about the afternoon of March 1st?"

"Yes. Steve and I had just gotten back to my parent's place in Renmus. Steve had been in court in Bremer because he'd been arrested for the marijuana the officer found in Jeff's car when Steve was driving it. Jeff came forward later, though, and admitted that the marijuana belonged to him. Anyway, when we got back to my house, Steve looked pretty upset, and when I gave him the keys to Jeff's car, I thought he might do something awful."

"Did you try to stop him?"

"I did, but he pushed me out of the way and took off. I knew that he just wanted to be alone to straighten things out with Jeff."

"Can you tell me what you did after Steve left?"

"I knew where Steve was headed, so I got in my car and followed him. He went to Hawkthorn like I thought he would. When I arrived in Hawkthorn, I headed right to Steve's house. I saw the Charger parked in front of the house, so I pulled up behind it and parked my car."

Jon was beginning to sink in his chair. The jury was on the edge of their seats. Everyone in the courtroom could see where I was headed with my questions. I was heading right for the heart of Jon's case, that Steve, in fact, had not been the shooter in the park.

"Beth, do you remember what you saw in the park?"

"Yeah. I saw Jeff at the far end of the park trying to egg Steve on. Steve kept heading toward him, and it sounded like Steve was trying to get Jeff to explain the marijuana thing."

"Why do you say that Jeff was trying to egg Steve on?"

"Because of what Jeff was yelling?"

"Do you remember what that was?"

"I'll never forget it. He was yelling, 'Come on, shoot me. You're too chicken too shoot me. You don't have the guts to do it.' Things like that."

"What did you think when you heard Jeff yelling those things?"

"It made me mad. I knew how mad Steve would get, and I could tell that Jeff was trying to get a reaction out of him. I thought that if I couldn't stop Steve, that he might actually try to shoot Jeff."

"Did you see Steve do anything?"

"Well, I saw him holding a pistol and pointing it at Jeff. Then I heard a gunshot and all I could think was oh, god, no."

Beth started to cry.

"Did you see Steve shoot the gun?"

"I don't think he did."

"Why do you say that?"

"Well, I never saw the gun move until Jason Windsor hit Steve. I think that if Steve had fired the gun, I would have seen it move or something in his hand."

"Besides the one shot, did you hear any other gun shots?"

"Yes. I definitely heard three shots total."

A small grin appeared on Hunlin's face. I could tell that he thought he was going to be able to use this latest line of questions to his advantage.

"Do you think that the shots were fired by Steve?"

"No."

I heard the whispers in the courtroom, and Judge Quinn slammed his gavel down again.

"This is your final warning! Go on, Jackson."

"Can you tell us why you don't think Steve fired the shots you heard?"

"Well, from where I was parked, I could see into the backyard of the house next to the Jones'. When I heard the first shot, I looked toward that backyard, and I saw a kid with a pistol. I watched him and I saw him fire twice more after I heard the first shot. He was shooting beer cans on the fence between the houses, but none of the cans moved. I think the shots were fired by him."

"Do you remember anything else?"

"Just the cops coming and arresting Steve and feeling sick to my stomach."

"Beth, I just have one more question for you. Did you tell all this to the county attorney?"

Looking very upset, Beth replied, "I tried. But no one would believe me. Jon Hunlin told me that they already had enough evidence to convict Steve and said he thought I was lying."

"I have no further questions, your honor."

Jon Hunlin looked speechless. The jurors were in shock, and the reporters were in a frenzy.

"Mr. Hunlin, cross examination?"

"Thank you, your honor."

Jon slowly pushed his chair back from the table and stood. He walked to his usual spot in the middle of the courtroom.

"Hello, Ms. Zable."

"Hello."

"You said you love Steve Jones, correct?"

"Yes, I do."

"You said you would do about anything to help Steve, didn't you?"

"I would."

"Are you sure that you saw the youngster in the yard?"

"I am."

"You're not just saying that to protect Steve are you?"

"I would never do that. I know that it's against the law to lie in court."

Jon walked back to his chair and sat down. He
paused for about ten seconds and a look of complete defeat
was starting to show on his face.

"I have nothing further."

"Okay, Beth, thank you for your testimony today.
You are free to go."

Beth left the witness box and walked toward the back
of the courtroom. She stopped when she reached Steve, and
the two of them gazed at each other for a moment as she
walked out of the courtroom. At least five reporters and
their camera crews followed quickly after her. Beth had
helped me launch my attack and set up my next witness.

Chapter XXX

"The defense calls Samuel Baxter."

Sam walked to the front of the courtroom, and he appeared to be very nervous. His parents were sitting in the courtroom and looked at him and tried to give him reassurance. Judge Quinn motioned for him to take a seat in the witness box and swore him in.

"Sam, my name is Judge Quinn."

"Hi."

"I want to tell you that it's really important that you tell the truth, okay? If you have any questions about anything you are asked, please let me know. Nothing is going to happen to you for telling the truth."

"I'll tell the truth your honor."

"Mr. Wright, you may proceed."

"Thank you, your honor."

"Hi, Sam. I'm Jackson Wright."

"Hi, Jackon. I remember talking to you before."

"You do?"

"Yes. You came and saw me and my parents this summer at our house in Hawthorn."

"Do you remember what we talked about before?"

"Yes."

"I'm going to ask you about that, okay?"

"Yes, sir."

"First of all, can you tell me where you live?"

"I live in Hawkthorn, across from the park, next to the Jones'."

"How long have you lived there?"

"My entire life. My parents have lived there even longer than that."

"What do you know about guns?"

"I know a lot about guns. My dad has taught me how to load them and shoot them. He's taking me rabbit hunting in a few weeks."

"Have you ever shot a gun in your backyard?"

I could see the same look of concern on Jon's face. He started to push his chair back to make an objection and then decided against it.

"Yes. My dad set up some targets in the backyard for me to shoot at. He said that it will help me become a better shot. I really want to get a rabbit this year."

"Do you shoot at the targets often?"

"Only when I think that it's safe; usually when nobody is around."

"Were you working on your target practice on March 1st."

"Yes. My dad had called me from work and said that I could go out back and practice as long as there was nobody else in the backyard. So I took his .22 caliber pistol and lined up my targets along the fence. I like the pistol 'cause it makes me feel like a cowboy."

"What were the targets that you set on the fence?"

"They were cans from my dad's beer can collection in our basement. They were old so I didn't think that he would care."

I nodded and looked toward the jury. Jon sat stunned, looking at Sam. His case was continuing to unravel.

"How many shots did you fire, do you remember?"

"I just shot three. After the third shot, I walked up to the cans to see if I hit any of them. While I was looking at the cans I heard sirens. I thought that I might get in trouble, so I ran inside the house. I knew that if I got in trouble, my dad would be mad."

"Why did you think that you might get in trouble?"

"My dad had said to be careful shooting in town because the cops could arrest me. So I thought that they were coming to look for me. I got scared and ran in the house and hid in my room."

"Did they come and look for you?"

"No. After about thirty minutes, I decided it was safe to look out our window. I saw that the police were talking to some guys in the park and realized that I wasn't going to get in trouble."

"Did you do anything else?"

"No."

"Did you tell anybody what happened?"

"Not until you came to my house. I was really scared and thought that I should keep it a secret because I didn't want to get in trouble."

"Thank you, Sam."

I took my seat as Hunlin got up to ask a few questions. He was scratching his head as he walked around the table. The courtroom was in a frenzy again, and I felt that the tide had definitely turned in my favor. Steve leaned over and said to me that he thought I was doing a very good job.

"Sam, do you remember seeing anything in the park the day you were taking target practice?"

"No. I didn't know that anything had happened in the park."

"Why didn't you tell me what you had done?"

"You never asked me."

Hunlin paused, trying to come up with more questions for Sam.

"I have no further questions."

A dejected Hunlin sat down. Judge Quinn looked at Sam, thanked him for coming to court and being so brave, and then told him he was free to go.

"Mr. Wright, do you have any other evidence?"

"No, your honor. The defense rests."

"If neither of the parties have any further evidence, We'll take a fifteen minute recess and then proceed to closing arguments."

Chapter XXXI

When we returned to court, Jon Hunlin rose and walked toward the jury box.

"Ladies and gentlemen of the jury, this is a very clear case of attempted murder. The evidence clearly shows that Steve Jones acted with malice to try to kill his brother Jeff. You heard eye witnesses testify that they heard the shots fired and saw Steve with the gun. The witnesses heard Steve yell at his brother that he was trying to kill him. Had it not been for the quick reactions of Stan Winfield and Jason Windsor, this would have been a murder trial and not an attempted murder trial. Steve was angry with his brother and sought revenge. He took the law in his own hands and proceeded without regard to the consequences. The only possible verdict for you to return in this matter is a verdict of guilty."

After Jon's very brief closing, he sat down, and I immediately walked to the front of the jury box so I could get the jury's full attention.

"I want to thank all of you for being so attentive to all the evidence that was presented to you. I just want to review the facts so that you're all clear on what actually happened in the park in Hawkthorn on March 1st. Steve Jones and Jeff Jones got into an argument. There was a lot of yelling. Steve was yelling at Jeff, and Jeff was yelling at Steve.

Jason Windsor knocked a gun from the hand of Steve Jones, and Stan Winfield wrestled Steve to the ground. The deputies arrived on the scene, arrested Steve Jones, did a quick investigation and left. What the county attorney and the deputies failed to tell you was that there were other witnesses they never bothered to interview. Also, the county attorney and the deputies knew that the possibility existed that another weapon had fired the shots but failed to investigate for another weapon. You all heard Beth's testimony that she saw another shooter in the area, and you all heard the shooter testify that he was firing a .22 caliber pistol, the same caliber as the bullets found in the park. Ladies and gentlemen of the jury, I ask you to consider all the evidence you have heard. Please review it completely, and after you have done that, if you have any doubt at all as to whether my client fired a gun at his brother, then you must find Mr. Jones not guilty of the charges against him. I am confident that when you have considered all the evidence, you will reach the only verdict that the evidence supports and which justice requires, a verdict of not guilty. Thank you."

I turned to walk back to the table and saw Steve watching me. When I sat down next to him, I said, "It is out of our hands now."

"Thank you, Jackson, for everything, but mostly for just believing in me."

I looked back to the bench to hear Judge Quinn's final instructions for the jury.

"This case is now submitted to the jury. I have prepared instructions for you, and I will ask you to review them carefully. You are only to take into consideration that evidence and testimony which was admitted. If you have any questions during your deliberation, please let me know, and I will help you out. Court will be adjourned until the jury reaches a verdict."

I walked out of the courthouse to a barrage of questions. For the first time since the case had started, I was willing to stop and try to answer the questions of the media.

"Do you think you won?"

I laughed and said, "That isn't up to me. The jury will decide who they believe, and I have faith that they will do the right thing."

"Can you tell us anything that wasn't presented in court?"

"No. What you saw is what you get. I thank you for your questions, but now I'm going to excuse myself and go home. I'm very tired."

The reporters continued to ask me questions as they walked alongside me to my car. When I got to the Saturn, I got in, rolled down the window, and said good bye.

Chapter XXXII

Judge Quinn's reporter called my office at 9:45 a.m. the next day and told Jill that the jury had reached a verdict. I packed up my briefcase and headed to Millsville. After the two week trial, I'd been relieved yesterday afternoon when Judge Quinn submitted the case to the jury for deliberation. The drive seemed interminable mostly because I spent those thirty minutes contemplating my client's future. The cornfields were filled with combines, harvest was in full swing, and the farmers were frantically working to complete their work before the winter snows began to fall. By the looks of the fields, this year's crop was going to be a bumper crop as long as the weather held. I reached the courtroom by 10:30 a.m. to find the Judge Quinn, Steve Jones, and Jon Hunlin all waiting for me.

"Good morning, your Honor."

"Good morning, Jackson. I'm glad that you were able to come over here so quickly. We have about five minutes until the jury will be brought in."

"Okay."

I sat down in my chair at the defense table and said hello to Steve. Words can hardly describe the anxiety I always feel in the moments before a jury returns with its verdict. Steve looked fairly relaxed, considering that the future of his life was about to be decided by twelve people he had never met before. Moments later, the jury was led in by the bailiff.

I always tried to study the jury as they walked into the courtroom. Four women and eight men walked into the jury box and took their seats. Judge Quinn greeted the jury, and they all said hello to him. I thought I saw juror number seven look over at my client but then I thought that might just be wishful thinking.

"Has the jury come to a verdict?"

"We have, your honor," said the foreman of the jury.

I was watching the back row of jurors to see if any of them would give me any additional reasons to believe that they were going to find my client not guilty. Both of the jurors sitting on the left end were ladies, and they both looked directly at me. I gave both of them a small smile and they both smiled back. A feeling of relief quickly came over me. I began to hope that the jury would find Steve not guilty. As I was beginning to relax and feel good about the reading of the verdict, I looked to the front row, and juror number three was looking directly at me. I looked back at him and gave him the same pleasant smile I had given the two other jurors. He looked back at me with disgust and shook his head. My feeling of calm was quickly replaced with feelings of major anxiety.

"Please hand your verdict to the bailiff."

The foreman of the jury stood up and waited for the bailiff to walk across the courtroom to the jury box. When the bailiff reached the jury box, the foreman reached out and handed him a folded piece of paper. The foreman sat back down and started to stare at his feet. I recognized that as a really bad sign. Another shot of anxiety hit me, and I thought that my stomach was going to explode. The bailiff walked from the jury box to the bench and handed Judge Quinn the folded piece of paper. Judge Quinn unfolded the paper and read it. He then looked down at my client and said, "Mr. Jones, will you please rise?"

Steve pushed back his chair and stood next to me. I took in a deep breath and slowly exhaled. I really could've used a smoke to help settle my nerves. Judge Quinn began to speak again.

"Mr. Foreman, State of Iowa v. Steve Jones, how does the jury find to the charge of attempted murder?"

The foreman looked up to the judge and said, "We, the jury, find the defendant, Steve Jones, not guilty of the charge of attempted murder."

I looked over at Steve, and he looked slightly relieved.

I nearly collapsed as I stood up. I extended my hand to Steve and as he reached out and shook it, he pulled me closer and gave me a giant hug.

"Thank you so much, Jackson."

"You're welcome, Steve. I'm glad that I was able to help you."

"You don't know how much this means to me. You've helped save my life and my future."

"I'm glad that I could help you, Steve."

The judge excused the jury, and they all departed from the courtroom.

He then said, "Do the parties have anything else for the court?"

Hunlin, looking dejected said, "No, your honor."

When Judge Quinn looked at me, I fought back the urge to smile and said, "No, your honor."

"Mr. Jones, on behalf of the State of Iowa, I would like to apologize. You are free to go, and your record will reflect that you were acquitted on all charges. I know that we cannot give you back the time you spent in jail but hope that, in time, you will be able to rebuild your life. Deputy, will you please come forward and remove Mr. Jones's handcuffs. Court is dismissed."

Deputy Kerns came forward and took the handcuffs from Steve Jones's wrists. I could see relief on Steve's face. His mother quickly rushed to the defense table and gave Steve a hug.

She looked at me and said, "Thank you so much for giving me back my son. It's been a very trying summer, and I can't wait to have him come home."

"I'm glad that I was able to help, ma'am."

She let go of Steve, and gave me a big hug, and began to cry.

"This means the world to me, Jackson. I don't know what I would have done if Steve had gone to prison after what happened to Jeff."

"Your family has been through a lot, and I'm so sorry about what happened to Jeff. Please let me know if you need anything."

"Thank you, Jackson. You certainly were an angel sent to my family."

Judge Quinn exited the courtroom, and I sat back down and stared up at the ceiling. The last fifteen minutes had meant that Steve Jones was leaving here a free man. Steve left the courtroom with his mother, their arms wrapped tightly and protectively around each other.

Chapter XXXIII

The scotch tasted good the night of the closing arguments of Steve's trial. I was just pouring myself a second glass of Dewars when my doorbell rang. I walked across the room to the door that led out to my balcony, and I looked down to see who it was.

"Hey, guys. Come on up."

I dropped my keys to Spencer and Lynn so they could let themselves in. The two of them joined me at the bar. This was starting to become an after work ritual for the three of us, and I definitely enjoyed it. No longer was I walking the streets visiting neighbors, they were now visiting me. It was a sign that I had become part of the community and that I had been accepted.

"What can I get you?"

"I'll just have a beer."

I reached under the bar and pulled a frosty mug from the freezer. I walked over to the keg fridge and poured a Boulevard for Spencer.

"Lynn?"

"How about a White Russian?"

"Coming right up."

"So, tell us what happened. You got the verdict in the Jones case today, right?"

I tried to shrug it off as no big deal.

"You know. Just the usual, not guilty."

"Jackson, everyone is talking about it."

"Really, Lynn?"

"Yeah. They're saying that it might affect Jon Hunlin."

"I really doubt that. Lacy Short would be lucky to find the courtroom, let alone try a case in it."

Apparently, news of the verdict had traveled quickly throughout the area. Spencer said that the talk in his office all day was that people couldn't believe that Jon hadn't been able to get a conviction on the attempted murder case.

I told them I hadn't thought he had much of a chance.

"Two of the key witnesses hadn't seen a thing. And without Jeff, the state's case was doomed."

"No kidding. Well, I'm glad it's over; it's worn you out."

"What do you say, tomorrow we hit the river?"

That sounded like a great idea to me. I had been trying to change the subject, but the only thing that Spencer was interested in was the Jones case.

"I hear that Jon Hunlin's afraid of you."

I chuckled, "As flattering as that is, I hardly think an attorney with thirty year's experience is afraid of me. He's more afraid of losing the election than he is of losing a trial to me."

"Maybe."

Spencer looked around the barroom, "You know what you need in here?"

"What?"

"Some of those old beer signs and a kick ass pool table."

"If I got a pool table, I'd never get rid of you."

Spencer laughed.

"Have you been out on the balcony yet?"

I had just had a local blacksmith build me a steel balcony. It had just been attached to the building last week.

"Nope."

"Let me grab my smokes, and we can step outside."

The two of us walked to the door and let ourselves out.

"So, what do you think of the view?"

Spencer laughed again. My balcony overlooked an alley. Across the alley were two dumpsters that were frequented by the neighborhood alley cats. Mars looked down on them daily and cursed them. The only thing you could see from my balcony were the tops of the neighboring buildings.

"I've been thinking of adding a spiral staircase that leads up to the top of the building. What do you think?"

"That would be pretty cool."

"I figure I could put a flower garden up there. It would give me the feeling of living in a big city."

It was amazing how we had all brought the flavor of the outside world back to Renmus with us. Spencer and Lynn had bought a house and remodeled it. The three of us were starting to spice up the town, and people were getting excited to be involved.

"So, what do you think?"

"I like it."

We headed back inside, and I poured the two of us a couple more drinks. Lynn had returned to the bar and had poured herself another drink.

"I see you found everything."

"Yep. You have this well stocked."

"I figured that if things didn't workout as a lawyer, I could always open up the bar to the community."

They both laughed and agreed that people would probably come just to see the renovations to the building. Most of what I had done to the second floor of the building was a mystery to the outside world. Just like everything else in Renmus, there was a fair amount of speculation about what my house looked like on the inside.

"You guys ever wonder how we ended up here?"

They both laughed again, "Almost every day."

It was the first time that I'd asked myself what type of future Renmus had to offer me. I knew that I had the opportunity to experience all kinds of great legal matters and that I had built an unbelievable practice. Still, I couldn't help but think that there was more in the world that I was meant to experience.

Chapter XXXIV

I met Chapman Wise in the same booking room I had met Steve in so many months earlier. He was sitting in the same chair and had that same look of fear on his face. Since it was late fall, I was wearing my warm topcoat. As I sat down, I pulled out a fresh pack of Marlboro Lights, opened them, and removed two cigarettes. I handed one to Chapman as I lit mine and then handed him my lighter so he could light his. This time I didn't bother to write down the questions I had for Chapman. I knew that it didn't really matter if any of the deputies were watching or listening to what we said.

"You know I can't do a lot for you, Chapman."

"I know. I really fucked up this time."

"What the hell were you thinking?"

"Well, I thought for sure that I could make it into the bank and back out without anyone really caring."

"Well, you're now looking at a whole new set of charges."

"That Stingray could really move."

"Chapman, I can probably get the new charges dropped, but you're going to have to agree to have your probation revoked."

"What if I don't agree to have my probation revoked?"

"Well, then, your choices are to fight the revocation of probation hearing and the new charges or you can volunteer to revoke your probation, and Jon Hunlin will drop the new charges against you."

"That's not an easy decision, Jackson."

"I know it isn't. But let's face it, you continue to fuck things up. Your deal was a good one."

Chapman was bouncing his right knee nervously and staring blankly at the floor just as Steve had the day he and I met.

"Okay. I want to go ahead and start serving my sentence."

I took a long drag off of my cigarette and looked at him.

"You know you'll get credit for the time you've spent in here and for the two days over in Rath County."

"Yes."

I started running some of the state prison term guidelines through my head. After a quick calculation I stated, "You should be up for parole in about two and a half years if you finish your associates degree program in jail and stay out of trouble in the pen."

Still bouncing his knee he said, "Thanks, Jackson, for everything."

I stood up and started to head for the door that lead out of the booking room.

"Well, I'm going to go see Judge Quinn so we can get this done right away."

When I left the booking room Deputy Martin was sitting at the front desk. I stopped to talk to him and asked him to bring Chapman over to the courtroom in about fifteen minutes.

I walked across the parking lot between the jail and the courthouse. Once inside the courthouse, I headed up to

Judge Quinn's chambers to ask if he could do a quick
revocation of probation hearing. Judge Quinn was always
very accommodating to the attorneys who practiced in his
court. As soon as I walked into his chambers and asked if he
could conduct the hearing, he agreed and asked me to have
my client brought over to the courtroom from the jail.

When I entered the courtroom, Chapman and Deputy
Martin were already seated inside. I motioned for Chapman
to join me at the defense table. His youth was quickly
starting to fade and the young man I'd met so many months
ago would quickly learn how to be a man in the state
penitentiary. I set my items on the table and ducked my head
into the law library to grab the county attorney. He was
sitting there sipping coffee.

"Judge Quinn is coming in to preside over a
revocation of probation hearing for Chapman Wise."

"I'll be right in."

The county attorney came walking in with the bailiff
about five minutes later. Chapman and I sat quietly. I didn't
really know what to say to him. I always tried to comfort a
man that was about to be sent to the big house, but I knew
even less of what to say to Chapman.

The bailiff said, "All rise. Court for Perkins County
is now in session. The Honorable Thomas Quinn presiding."

Everyone in the courtroom stood and waited for
Judge Quinn to arrive. As the judge entered, Chapman was
noticeably shaking.

"Please, be seated."

"Mr. Wright, it is my understanding that your client
wishes to have his probation revoked. Is that correct?"

"Yes, your honor."

"Does the state wish to say anything."

"No."

"Mr. Wright, do you wish to say anything on behalf
of your client?"

"Your honor. Mr. Wise is a young man who has made more than one mistake in his young life. He is not resisting the State's motion to revoke his probation, and he is prepared to leave from court to begin serving his sentence."

"Mr. Wise, do you have anything to add?"

"No, your honor. Just that I am terribly sorry for what I have done."

"I then find that the State's grounds for its motion to revoke probation is founded and will enter an order revoking your probation. You will be transported to the Iowa State Correctional Facility to begin serving your sentence for assault. You were convicted of this crime just two days ago. You were originally given a suspended sentence for this crime, however, your actions yesterday leave me no choice but to rule this way. Do the parties have anything else for the court?"

Both the county attorney and I replied, "No, your honor."

Judge Quinn left the courtroom and so did the county attorney. Another victory for Jon Hunlin, and his campaign for re-election was looking better every day. The news of Steve Jones being acquitted had filled the air waves that morning and was Tom Clark's lead story.

Watching Deputy Martin lead Chapman out of the courtroom, my heart sank. I had done all that I could for him and now he was going to the state penitentiary for ten years. I gathered up my files, notepad and pen and headed out of the courtroom trying to figure out why good kids make bad choices. Steve Jones and Chapman Wise had many of the same traits, both being young, reckless and care free. Today had been just another day of being an advocate for my client.

Walking with these boys through their journey to manhood set the tone for my enjoyment of small legal victories that are as short lived as the flight of eagles.